# Swim For Your Life

## Don Bailey

Parts of this book have appeared in *Prairie Fire, Lunatic Gazette* and *West Coast Review* and have been read on CBC Anthology and Celebration. Preparation of the manuscript was made possible by grants from the Canada Council and the Ontario Arts Council.

ISBN 0 88750 546 5 (hardcover)
ISBN 0 88750 547 3 (softcover)

Cover art by Herzl Kashetsky. Typesetting and design by Michael Macklem

Printed in Canada

PUBLISHED IN CANADA BY OBERON PRESS

This book is for, and because of, Angela.

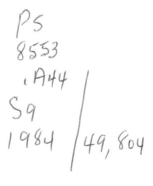

# The Final Approach

As the two attendants strap Gloria into the portable cot, she
wonders if the hot-plate has been turned off. She can see it
sitting on the kitchen counter just inches below the small
cupboard that holds the few dishes she bought at the Crip-
pled Civilians store. She imagines the element becoming
red hot and then the paint, the innumerable coats on the
old cupboard, begin to blister, and then the wood starts to
smolder. And then the flames. Fire spills through the two-
room apartment like a giant wave and everything is des-
troyed. Even Mrs. Goose, her favourite stuffed creature,

5

perched primly on the orange crate beside her bed, wearing a ruffled maid's cap and matching apron, has vanished. A great sense of loss engulfs her. She would like to warn someone of the potential tragedy or at least weep for it, but she is numb. Everything is like a dream. The way she likes it.

Gloria is aware of being carried down two flights of stairs. She hears the men grunting as they load her into the ambulance, but as the vehicle lurches into the traffic, its siren sounding, her mind becomes scrambled in its sense of location. She feels the panic of being in a darkened, empty theatre. The movie is finished. The spell of being anchored in her fantasy is broken. But suddenly, the flickering picture of her father moves onto the screen and a new story begins.

The two of them are flying safely through the air in his plane. She knows he is terrified of heights and imagines that his hands are sweating as he handles the controls and listens intently to the instructions from the controller in the tower. But he betrays no fear. He is the perfect actor. He reveals only what the script calls for. When two Canada geese appear near the wing in a manner that suggests that they want to hitch a ride, Gloria would like to shout with excitement, wave, something, but she notes that her father's reaction to the astounding sight is a mere nod of acknowledgement in their direction, as if their appearance was for his benefit. He has the knack of making the astonishing seem ordinary and familiar. No earthly event seems capable of shaking his confidence. She is envious of his poise. She vows to be like that herself one day. Unthreatened and distant. She imagines her father's life is painless.

A sudden updraft bounces the small aircraft and frightens her. Her father calmly adjusts the flaps to bring the bumping under control while Gloria concentrates on the clumps of small clouds. They remind her of the bowls of leftover bread pudding that seemed to fill the shelves of her mother's refrigerator when she was a child. But where are the raisins? Her mother always used tons of them. So perhaps the clouds were just clouds or, more likely, floating chunks of plasticene waiting to be shaped. Gloria is embarrassed by these childish thoughts. She never wants her father to know she has such frivolous thoughts or that many things frighten her.

The tower has given them landing clearance. They are in the final approach. The dropping plane causes her stomach to flutter. She tries to focus on the landscape but the forms of trees and buildings blur into an image of jumpy motion that makes her feel sick. The wheels touch the runway for a second but then the aircraft lurches away from the ground. The seat-belt bites into her swollen belly and the pain of it makes her gasp. She imagines the baby inside her being twisted into some grotesque shape. They bump down again and this time the wheels find a grip and they roll with ever-decreasing speed toward the hangar. When they have finally stopped, Gloria's father puts his hand in hers. It is hot and sweaty. She is startled by the heat and looks to his face for other signs, but it is set in a serene smile. She suspects that flying frightens him, but he persists. If she were to ask him, he would tell her that fear, like this flimsy airplane, must be controlled. Otherwise there would be a crash.

And then he is gone. He never waits for her to form the questions she needs to ask. She feels the anger build and burst from her mouth in a scream of rage.

"Daddy!"

She feels a cold instrument touching her belly. A young doctor is shining a light in her eyes. The baby shifts and the twist of pain makes her giggle. How preposterous for her to even dream that she might have control over anything. She hears voices and knows that they are talking about her.

7

She can tell by the tone. The words are too far away.

"Valium," the ambulance attendant says. "She had a prescription. We found the container. Looks like she took them all."

"Couldn't have been too many. Her respiration is good," the doctor says. "The baby doesn't seem to be in jeopardy. We monitor them both. Until morning anyway."

"Daddy," Gloria moans. Vaguely she feels regret. She is sorry for all this. She is glad she is alone in whatever new shame this may be. She is grateful her father was not here to hear her cry out. She knows how he hates to be called Daddy.

An IV is poked into her arm and she is moved to the psychiatric unit.

In another part of the city, Gloria's father wanders about in his apartment watering the plants. He is wearing his dead wife's housecoat. It is far too tight and has torn at the armpits from his stretching, but it contains the smell of her. It is the last thing that belonged to his wife that he has not given away or thrown out. He knows that by keeping the garment he is prolonging the agony of her absence, but he is not ready to give up the pain. The pain is a link with living. He is afraid to let go.

Wayne Maitland is 42 years old and unsure of why he is alive. Wanda, his wife, had been 34. Clearsighted in her vision of the future, she scrambled forward relentlessly, claiming all territory she touched as her own. He followed, unthinking, concerned only with setting a pace for himself that would keep him caught up. When the lump appeared on Wanda's breast, she reacted with irritation, as if she had contracted a nasty case of measles. Even after the surgery, followed by chemotherapy, she refused to believe in the possibility of her own death. Her determined resistance to the truth was rewarded with a three-month remission. She

8

hardly seemed to notice the evidence of recurrence. When the deadly cycle finally claimed her, Wayne was stunned. She had never let him down before.

The apartment is too big for him and the boy. Three bedrooms and a study. Wayne imagines someone living with them. A woman, alone like himself, with a child about George's age. Six or seven. The children could be buddies and play together. There were bunk beds in George's room. And she could have the big bedroom. It had its own bathroom and a huge closet with a mirrored door where Wanda would watch herself as she modeled a new dress he had bought. Perhaps the new woman would erase the lingering reflection of Wanda. He would use the spare bedroom. He wouldn't mind. They could share the costs and some of the cooking and shopping. They could spell each other off with the children. It would be company.

He imagines it all like a movie he has written. Each scene is worked out to the last detail. Every day he scans the want-ads for people looking to share accommodation, as if he were a director casting the parts. But no-one fills the bill. Or at least none of the ads seem to have the right tone, so he never calls. He would really prefer someone to call him.

The phone rings as he soaks another avocado tree. There are twenty such trees around the apartment. Wayne thinks of himself as being a bit of an expert on the fruit. He picks each one carefully from a bin at the local market, making sure they are just the right degree of ripeness. At home, he peels off the tough skin and puts the pulp in the blender with several garlic cloves, a drop of oil and lots of sour cream. A few seconds of swirling and he has the perfect salad-dressing. On occasion he leaves out the oil and the concoction is thick and tangy, perfect for dipping potato chips, an activity George and he enjoy while they watch television. Sometimes the two of them even make sandwiches out of the stuff. The large pits of the fruit are dried and then rooted in water. Later they are transferred to pots of soil where with lots of trimming they grow into short, bushy trees. Wayne is proud of them, of his ability to coax visible growth from something that looks dead. If nothing else, he sometimes thinks, I can grow avocado pits.

The phone rings persistently. It is almost midnight and Wayne does not want George woken. He hesitates before picking up the receiver, hoping the ring will stop. He does not like late-night calls. It rings again and he answers it.

"Yes," he says cautiously.

"Toronto General Hospital calling," a woman says. "Is this Mr. Wayne Maitland?"

"Yes."

"This is Head Nurse Hendrich. I'm calling about your father. Thomas Maitland."

"What's happened?" Wayne asks, tensing himself for a death report.

"He just signed himself out," the woman says.

"But he can't! He's too sick! I just saw him last week."

"We know his condition, but he insisted. He called a cab from the nursing-station and said he was going to his son's house. I thought I should warn you."

"But I can't take care of him. He was getting injections twice a day."

"He's taking his medication orally now," she says. "In fact he's perked up quite a bit in the last few days. His doctor was talking about releasing him."

"Well, thank you for calling," Wayne says, and he hangs up.

He begins the ritual of preparing for a guest. He lights the kindling in the fireplace and piles a couple of logs on the flames. A fresh pot of coffee is started and a bottle of whisky, along with a bucket of ice and some glasses, is put within easy reach on the coffee-table. Wayne pours himself a small glass of the liquor and sips it as he stares out the window watching for the man who is his father. Outside it is snowing. A fierce wind blows the stuff in swirling clouds through the park across the street. Wayne can hear the radio playing softly in the background. It's an FM station broadcasting a tribute to Hank Williams. The music is sad, melancholy, a kind of musical litany but void hope. Wayne considers turning it off but there is something soothing and even reassuring about hearing the depths of another man's depression. Perhaps his father will like it. Wayne realizes the next hour would be easier if the person coming were a total stranger. He would know how to act. His father is a frightening mystery who seems now, at this late stage, to want something from Wayne. Wayne cannot imagine what that might be. He wonders if he is capable of responding to whatever request his father might have. Or if he wants to.

"Mummy!"

Wayne runs up the stairs to George's room. The boy is thrashing around under the covers, his legs kicking at the blankets. He is on his back and his small hands are closed in tight fists that he pounds against the bed. Wayne takes him in his arms and cradles him against his chest. George lets out a loud wail and then cries softly. Wayne rocks him gently until the boy opens his eyes.

"I seen her," he says. "And she had the mask on. She couldn't talk."

"It's okay," Wayne says. Wanda has been dead for eight months but still the nightmares haunt the boy.

"I wanted her to talk," George says.

The doorbell rings.

"Who's there?" George asks.

"Probably my father," Wayne says.

"Grandpa! Can I see him? How come he's here?"

"It's late. He's left the hospital. I don't know what he wants."

"Just for a minute, Dad. I hardly ever see him."

"Are you okay now?"

"It was just a dream," the boy says.

Only seven, but already George can cement over the holes of horror that have been punched into his life. Wayne regrets this ability but knows of no other remedy.

"You can come down for a minute. But just a minute."

The boy scrambles out of bed and the two of them go downstairs. The doorbell is being pushed persistently and the sound fills the apartment. Wayne opens the door and has to step out of the path of the rushing body.

"About time. It's freezing out."

The man shakes off the snow, shrugs out of his shapeless coat and tosses an old canvas bag among the winter boots.

"Hello, Dad," Wayne says, reaching out awkwardly to embrace the man. His father tolerates the contact for a brief second and then pulls away.

"Let me get my rubbers off at least," he says. He struggles to bend and his face shows pain. Finally he just kicks them off. He sees George standing behind Wayne but makes no sign of recognition.

"So who's the midget," he says as he takes a seat on the couch near the fire.

"It's me!" George shouts. He runs toward the man and scrambles into his lap.

"You know me, Grandpa."

"Didn't recognize you with them ears. Looks like a couple of winter mitts growing out of your head." He laughs at his joke and begins to tickle the boy.

"No. No." George protests and the old man finally stops.

"Are my ears really that big?" George asks.

"Naw, probably just your head shrunk," his grandfather

says.

George looks worried and puts his hands up to his ears to feel their size. Thomas Maitland wraps his arms around the boy and hugs him tightly.

"Only kidding you, Georgy," he says. "Hey anyway, what are you doing up so late? Haven't you got school tomorrow?"

"He sure has," Wayne says. "He just wanted to say hello."

"Are you gonna stay with us, Grandpa?" George asks.

"I've got to talk to your dad."

"You could sleep in the lower bunk," George offers. "I always sleep on the top. My dad won't mind. Lots of times I have friends stay over."

Wayne is uneasy with this talk. His father is ill. Thin and frail. He needs taking care of. This is not a task that Wayne feels is his responsibility. He has no wish to tend to this man who has never demonstrated a willingness to do the same for him. He might be called father but he's never earned the benefits that go with the name. How can a man who has never shared his life with you ask you to share his death? Wayne wanted no part of it.

"Give Grandpa a kiss, George. And then it's up to bed," he says.

George delivers a wet kiss on the mouth of the old man, who pushes him away in embarrassment.

"Go on with you," he says.

At the stairs George stops and turns back.

"Have you got cancer like my mummy?" he asks.

"I'm none too good," the old man says, "but I'm not dead yet."

"Come on to bed," Wayne urges.

"See you in the morning, Grandpa," George says.

After he tucks him in, Wayne stands by the bed for a few moments holding George's hand. The boy quickly finds sleep and Wayne goes downstairs.

"Pour me a shot of that rye, will you," his father asks.

"What about your medicine? Won't it . . . "

"Stopped taking it this morning. Stuff just made me sleep. No ice. Just the booze."

Wayne shrugs and does as he is told. The old man drinks half of it in one swallow and lets out a sigh of satisfaction.

"Now that's what I call medicine," he says.

"You've come here, Dad," Wayne says. "I figure you want something."

"You're not working still, eh?" his father says.

"I told you. I'm on sabbatical this year."

Wayne teaches script-writing for film, but after his wife's death the head of the department arranged for him to take the rest of the year off. The college had no obligation to him since he wasn't tenured. He was still surprised at how well they had treated him. Sometimes though, he wished he was back in the classroom. There were days when he felt like a rusty, inoperative machine. He believed there could be no joy in living without purpose. And for him that meant having work to do. Real work.

"You writing another one of those pictures?"

"I'm fooling around with some ideas."

"I hope it's better than that last one. What was it called, Feast of Something?"

"Feast of Rage," Wayne says.

"People don't want to see pictures like that. All of that blood and violence and everybody hating everybody. Why don't you write something nice?"

"That film grossed twice what it cost to make. People like slice-and-dice films."

"They pay you a lot of money?"

"Pretty good."

"You don't act rich."

"Well, I'm not."

"But you've got that airplane. That must have set you back."

"It's just an old crate."

The plane is a Piper Warrior, four-passenger with retractable landing-gear. A beautiful, sleek aircraft. Wayne keeps it at the island airport. The upkeep and hangar space he rents is expensive, but he needs to know it is there any time the desire for escape takes hold of him. No-one has ever flown with him. It is his private diversion. He is terrified of heights and flying scares him, but the battle with his fear is worth the sense of relief and accomplishment he feels when he lands after another flight. And there is a feeling of exhilaration that comes with the realization that he is alone among the clouds. Sometimes he cries with grief for the loss of Wanda. He weeps for himself and George, alone and uncharted without her. He mourns the brevity of her life, the things left undone that she felt passionately about. But at other times he sings, his voice raised loudly to the tunes of his youth, in a strange spell of elation. These temporary sojourns away from the earth have become a necessity. The day after Wanda's coffin was lowered into the ground, he had begun flight instruction. Otherwise, he was sure he would have gone crazy.

"Why did you leave the hospital?" Wayne asks.

"I figured I could come and give you a hand."

Wayne laughs at the absurdity of the idea.

"Don't laugh," the old man says. "I'm a good cook. I cooked in the army. I could do the cleaning-up around here. You could get back to work. Stop all this moping around."

"I'm not moping around."

"Sure you are. It's not healthy for your son. Pour me another shot of that stuff."

15

Wayne hands the bottle to the old man, who pours several inches into his glass.

"That stuff can't be good for you," Wayne says.

"You know what I've got?" the old man asks.

"Cancer."

"That's right. Of the pancreas. It's slow. It'll kill me for sure, but don't worry about me dying on your doorstep. I'll be out of here long before that. In the meantime, I can give you a hand here in return for my room and board."

"You've got it all figured out."

"Is it a deal?"

The old man holds his hand out and Wayne takes it but does not return the urgent shake meant to seal the bargain. Instead he holds its roughness and remembers how often as a boy he had longed to have this hand holding his. But there had been the war. And then his father had worked on the boats and been away. Wayne had experienced the absence of that hand all his life. It had created in him a longing for something he had never known. And now that same hand was being offered to bind him to a deal he didn't want.

"I'm not destitute," Thomas Maitland says, pulling his hand away. "I've got my pension. I can get a room. I thought I'd be a help to you."

"We'll try it and see how it works out," Wayne says.

"I don't want you doing me any special favours," his father says.

"You're my father."

"And grandfather to that boy up there!"

Wayne laughs at the transparent clinging to this tentative family connection. But Wayne recognizes, behind the fierce statement, his father's fear. He knows such fear himself and thinks perhaps then there can be a bond. The bonding fear of being alone.

"You're a tough old guy," he says.

16

"I'm 68 and I'm damned if I'm going to let them drain away what's left of me with their tubes and needles."

"The bed's made up in the spare room," Wayne says. "I'll see you in the morning."

"Thanks, son," Thomas Maitland says.

Wayne goes up the stairs slowly, wondering about his lack of generosity. He resents the intrusion of his father, of the sickness and prospect of death he brings. He resents having to remember the pain his father's absence once gave him. Wayne is afraid closeness will be demanded of him. He is determined to avoid it. Intimacy, he believes, is the meanest trick that life plays because it never, never lasts.

Wayne finds momentary peace in deep sleep. The inner winds of turmoil, like the weather outdoors, have calmed during the night. He is stirred into consciousness by the sound of the ringing phone. He hears George downstairs answer it. He feels a fleeting second of pride in the boy who now makes his own breakfast.

"It's for you, Dad!" George calls up. "Some hospital."

Wayne groans. He assumes they are calling about the old man. He imagines himself having to handcuff his father and drag him back to the hospital. The prospect does not please him. He picks up the phone beside his bed.

"Hello."

"Mr. Wayne Maitland?"

It's a woman's voice. Somehow familiar.

"Mr. Maitland, this is Dr. Sharon Sheaney. We've spoken before. I'm calling about Gloria."

"Gloria!"

"Yes, Gloria, your daughter. Did I wake you up, Mr. Maitland?"

"What's wrong?" Wayne asks, ignoring the sarcasm.

"Another suicide flirtation. This is the third time in six months, Mr. Maitland. It was pills again. Thank God it was

17

only valium. I want to see you this morning. We have to talk."

"I'll be there," Wayne says and he hangs up.

After breakfast he walks George to school. The air is cold and still. A light snow falls. George slides on the icy sidewalks.

"Is Grandpa going to come and live with us?" he asks.

Wayne wonders. Perhaps this is the time to move. To leave Toronto for a safer place. Somewhere like Winnipeg. He could get a job teaching there. Probably he could. Sell all their possessions, pack their clothes into the plane and fly away. Leave all this. Let the tragedies of others marinate in their own misery. He laughs aloud as he realizes he is beginning to sound like a maudlin poet. Perhaps it really is time to write another horror film. He has been playing with an idea for a story in which there is only one character alive. Everyone else is a ghost. The problem is that the man who is alive believes that he is dead. He feels he owes an explanation to the others but they won't listen. This is his hell. In the end he kills himself and suddenly he is in contact with the others. They listen to what he has to say, his apologies, his confessions. They are amused at his belief that he has restored himself to life by his ritual act of suicide. They inform him that his secrets mean nothing because, as the dead, they can change nothing. The last image that Wayne thinks of is that of a man flying a small plane through an endless bank of cloud, searching for a clear patch of sky through which he can spot the earth and find a place to land.

The trouble with this story, Wayne thinks, is that it sounds like a morality play. Full of judgments and delusions, but no blood or gore. Ghosts don't bleed.

"Is he gonna?" George persists.

"I don't know," Wayne answers. "He's going to stay for

a little while. Then we'll see."

"I hope he stays with us for ever and ever," George says.

"How come?" Wayne asks.

"Because he loves me."

"How do you know that?"

"I just do," the boy says.

As they enter the schoolyard, Wayne stops and scoops George up in what he recognizes as a desperate embrace.

"I love you too," he says.

"I know that," George says and he wriggles free and runs off to join his playmates.

Maybe the dead are like snowflakes, Wayne thinks as he slowly walks home. Falling from the sky to remind us of their presence. Their cold existence ephemeral as they touch and melt against our faces. Like frozen ashes. It is not an unpleasant thought. Wayne imagines building a snowman in the back yard in the shape of Wanda. He sees himself lifting the snow figure from the ground and holding it in his arms. He hears music and begins to move. They are dancing. He is sure he can hear her gay laughter and the tears that flow from his eyes blur the picture in his mind until it fades into a grey haze. He quickens his step, his eyes blinking against the snowflakes.

An hour later, he is sitting in the office of Dr. Sharon Sheaney. She is a psychiatrist, about 35 and head of the crisis unit. Wayne is intimidated by her. Her hair is long and always in disarray. Her eyes sparkle with intelligence and then, unpredictably, flash with rage. Wayne has no control over her. She ignores the polite conversation he generates to help make things easier between them. She reminds him of a film editor who cuts out all the lovely lyrical background, the mood-setting shots, saving only the action sequences.

"I'm seriously thinking of doing an involuntary commital," she says. "At least until after the baby's born."

"That's pretty drastic," Wayne says.

"Yes, it is. You offer me another choice."

"Me! What am I supposed to do?"

"Take her home with you," she says. "Your wife's dead. You've got a small child. She could help you. You could help each other. She's not stupid you know."

A powerful feeling of helplessness overcomes Wayne. The energy drains from him. He knows he will never be able to explain to this woman why he cannot cope with his daughter.

"We're so different," he says.

"That's crap! She adores you. Worships you. There's nothing she wants more than to be just like you. The more you reject her, the more she clamours for your attention."

"I don't like the blame being put on me," Wayne says.

"Sure you don't, but your ex-wife won't take any responsibility. You won't take any. Who's the kid supposed to turn to?"

"She's old enough to make her own decisions."

"Have you noticed how good she is at it?"

"I feel sorry for her," Wayne says and then anger takes hold of him. "And I don't need you to guilt-trip me about her. I give her money, set her up in an apartment. Even buy groceries for her. I can't live her life for her."

"You do everything but the most important thing, Mr. Maitland."

"What's that?"

"You refuse to include her in your life."

"How do I explain to my seven-year-old son if she goes into her suicide act?"

"I don't know. That's the risk you take."

"She's eighteen. She made her choice two years ago when she moved in with her boyfriend. I begged her to stay. My wife was sick. I needed help then."

The doctor glares at him, her mouth stretching into a grimace.

"Next you'll be saying, she made her bed and now she has to lie in it. I credited you with more creativity. Tell me, Mr. Maitland, what age do our children have to be before we're no longer responsible for them,"

Wayne is furious at her manipulation. He has enough guilt without this woman adding to the heap of garbage rotting inside him, emitting poison through his system.

There is a soft tapping on the door.

"Come in," the doctor says.

Gloria enters. She looks at her father and he turns away.

"I'm sorry, Father," she says.

"What are you apologizing to him for?" the doctor asks.

Wayne gets up and helps Gloria ease into a chair. He pats her shoulder and remains standing, close to her.

"You okay?" he asks.

"Still a little groggy," she says.

She looks up at his worried face. Guilt chills her body. Some day, she thinks, they will meet differently. Like old friends bumping into each other who have not seen each other for years. And they will hug each other with pleasure and ask caring questions. For some reason she remembers sitting at the kitchen table when she was very young and this man, her father, showing her how to trace pictures from magazines. She sees his grin as she completes the first picture that she did entirely on her own. He is smiling proudly at her learning and his teaching. She is sure he loved her then.

"The situation we have here . . . " the doctor begins.

Wayne steps in front of Gloria, facing her.

"Do you want to come home with me?" he asks.

"If you want me," she answers.

21

"My father is staying with George and me. He's sick. Dying, I guess."

He doesn't know why he is doing this. The doctor is watching him carefully. It is as if he has flown too high and the oxygen has thinned, making him giddy and uncertain of his flight path. He feels reckless.

"Maybe I could help," Gloria says and then she laughs lightly. "I am a bit limited with this caboose I've got growing here."

Wayne smiles and lets a choking giggle escape.

"What's funny?" the doctor asks.

"Everybody wants to help," Wayne says.

"Do you think you can let them?" she asks.

"If we run into problems, I'll call," Wayne says.

"I'll be here," she says.

Gloria struggles out of her chair and for a brief second she pushes herself against Wayne in an affectionate nuzzle. It is too fast for him to respond. She hurries from the room to get her coat and Wayne turns to the doctor feeling embarrassed. She has seen his stiff self. He would like her to know that he's a dancer too. That, on occasion, he can leap into the air and be suspended in happiness. He would like her to know that he is like everyone else, a mixture of emotions struggling for balance. Sometimes raging and at other times overcome with unexplainable serenity.

"You're smiling again," the doctor says.

"I was thinking that I'd like it if you could somtimes see me differently."

"I already have," she says.

Gloria returns. Some of the fear she feels shows in the way her eyes are squinted. She looks to the doctor for instructions. None are forthcoming, so instead she reaches out her arm to circle her father's waist. She even leans on him a little and there is no resistance. She feels him attempt to get his arm around her but the bulk of the soon-to-be-born baby makes it impossible. She laughs nervously and her father joins her. They leave like that, awkward, fearful but together, with the doctor calling after them.

"Try to get along."

The following Saturday morning found all four Maitlands sitting at the kitchen table finishing breakfast. Gloria observes this typical family scene with a sense of wonder. The atmosphere is restful, the way she imagines it would be in a real family. She cannot explain it but she feels the baby within her is somehow responsible.

"I'll tell you," Thomas Maitland says, "cleaning that fireplace was some job. No wonder the thing didn't draw. When was the last time you cleaned it, Wayne?"

Wayne is hiding behind the newspaper. He peeks over at his father and is surprised at how well he looks. The man has cancer. Terminal. How can he be so active? He naps a lot but the rest of the time he's always busy with something. Taking George skating. Cleaning out the clothes-closets. Even doing some of the shopping. Wayne marvels at his father's determination and he wonders if his own measures up.

"I never cleaned it," Wayne answers.

"Well, I could've told you that," Thomas Maitland says. "Lucky you didn't smoke yourself out."

"I put the roast out for supper," Gloria says. "We're going to have broccoli and mashed potatoes."

"With gravy?" George asks.

Wayne listens and is himself part of this ordinary talk. He feels satisfied with the way things are for the moment. A few days before he started a new film-script. It is not a horror story this time. The story is about children and even has a dog in it. It will be a director's nightmare but this doesn't concern Wayne. He is excited about trying to write

23

a happy story.

Gloria looks at her father's eyes. He does not notice her watching him. She likes to do this sometimes. It's like she's spying on him when he thinks he is in private. She sees less sadness in him now. She believes that when the child comes he will be ready to receive it with the affection she once had. She thinks he will be a wonderful grandfather.

"Just think," Thomas Maitland says. "Another month and I'll be a great-grandfather. I never thought I'd live to see it."

"What're we going to do today?" George asks.

Wayne ignores this. He is happy to float aimlessly in his imagination. Images of Wanda appear and he smiles back at his memories of her.

"He's kicking," Gloria says.

"Let me feel," Thomas Maitland says. And he places his hand gently on Gloria's belly.

"Me too," George says. And he runs from his chair to Gloria's side. Cautiously he places his small hand next to his grandfather's.

"He's really there!" George shouts. "I felt him move. He's kicking to get out."

Wayne is startled, pulled back from the edge of his dreams where he was flying alone in a perfect sky. He looks at his daughter and he knows she is waiting. He reaches out, suddenly unafraid, and he feels the new life move under his hand. He laughs out loud.

"You're right. He's there."

Gloria puts her hand over her father's. She looks boldly into her eyes and he meets her gaze. She sees what might be tears. She does not know if he is glad or sad. Perhaps she will never know what he feels, but it is enough for now to imagine a time when they are closer. A time when she will be able to reveal to him all the things inside her that make her who she is. She feels his hand sliding away and watches as he looks out the window at the clear, cold day. Everything is still outside. Calm.

"I have an idea," Wayne says. "It looks like a perfect day for flying. Anybody want to come?"

The family sits in surprised silence. He gets up and goes to the phone. Inside he is shaking. It is as if a frozen surface has been broken through by the surging water underneath. He dials the number of the airport with slow, deliberate movements. He hears the ring and then someone answers.

"I'm calling," he says, "to check the weather report. It looks like a perfect day for flying."

He can hardly hear the voice confirming the ideal conditions for the shouting and excited laughter of his family in the background.

## Late in the Game

It is not a desire for sex that pushes him to make the call.
He would like some sex. God, yes. A bouncing, sweaty romp
with somebody. Somebody nice. Somebody who would tell
him he was a generous lover. Someone who would make
him breakfast and scratch his back while he ate it. He didn't
know anyone like that. Wayne Maitland is 42 years old and
afraid. He is afraid of dying. He makes the call because it
is daring and even dangerous. Perhaps it will help keep him
alive. The excitement makes his hands shake as he dials
the number. A bored woman's voice asks for his Visa num-

ber. He has the card ready and gives it to her. She tells him
he will be billed 37.50 and then gives him another phone
number. Now that he is a member, she says, he can call the
number any time he wants. He is disappointed. He thought
she would be the one. He hangs up the phone and lights a
cigarette. He thinks of his dead wife, Wanda. She would
find this situation hilarious. Her laughter hovers over him
like a case of hiccups. The fear begins to sweep over him
and he quickly picks up the magazine and stares at the picture of the woman in the advertisement. Her legs are spread
and she is cupping her large breasts in her hands. There is a
caption that says: call me. He calls.

A warm but slightly bored woman answers.

"This is Brenda Lee. Ya got three minutes to get off on
the phone. Say anything and I'll listen."

Wayne is seized with laughter.

"Brenda Lee!" he chokes.

"What's wrong with that? She used to be the greatest.
You don't think I'm going to say my real name."

"How did you know . . . what I was calling about?"

"I got a special phone. Everybody who calls me on that
one is looking for the same thing. So you go ahead. Ya already wasted a minute."

"It says in the ad that I can talk as long as I want."

She laughs loudly and with relish. Obviously this is a
subject she has some investment in. She no longer sounds
bored.

"Sure that's what it says. But that's all bullshit 'cause they
only pay me 2.00 a call and if you can't get off in three minutes then, you know, I might be on the phone all night with
ya. No good for me."

"How come three minutes?"

There is a second or two of hesitation.

"I got one of those egg-timers," she says. "When a call

**27**

comes I turn it over and watch. When it's finished you should be too."

"You mean one of those hour-glass kind?" Wayne asks.

"Yeah."

"I haven't seen one of those since I was a kid."

"I found it at the church rummage sale. Say, you gonna talk up or what? Your time is running down. Oh shit, hang on . . . ."

She bangs down the receiver and in the background he can hear the voices of squabbling children.

"I don't care what Freddie says," he hears her say. "Youse guys ain't gonna watch any spooky shows."

Wayne begins to get a picture of her. Probably she is wearing a housecoat. One that needs to be replaced. Her hair is up in curlers because she wants to look nice for the week but she can't afford the hairdresser. He wonders if she has a husband.

"Hey, mister . . . mister. You one of those breather guys?"

"Sorry, I was day-dreaming," Wayne says.

"Well, I turned the timer over. Ya can start again. It wasn't your fault. About the kids."

"They're up pretty late."

A pause of silence.

"You sound like one of those welfare people. You ain't from the welfare, are ya?"

For an instant there is real panic in her voice and then the laughter begins again.

"Listen to myself. I'll tell ya though. They watch ya like a hawk. Say, you got nothing dirty you want to say to me?"

"I guess not," Wayne says.

"I don't get many talkers," she says. "I mean just talk. Some of those guys say real garbage to me. It gets me mad sometimes."

"Why do you do it?"

"Mister, the same as everybody does everything. Money. Two boys cost a lot of money. But I'll tell ya. During the week, right to bed. Never sauce me back. So on the weekends it's kind of a treat I give them. Staying up late."

"You on your own? No husband?"

"Now, don't go gettin' too inquisitive," she says coyly, and then her voice flattens out. "Naw, the bastard's gone. He came back once four years ago. Stayed three months. That's how I got the youngest. I really thought he was going to stay."

"I'm on my own too," Wayne says.

"Wife run off?"

"She died," Wayne says. "Cancer."

"Oh, that's terrible. You don't sound that old either. And did she leave you with kids?"

"One. A boy. He's six. George is his name."

"That sounds so grown up. Must be a comfort though, having him."

"Most of the time," Wayne says.

"Oh, I know," she says laughing. "They can get on your nerves too. But it's nice to know they're there just the same."

"I guess I better go," Wayne says.

"Sure," she says. "And you call any time. You got a nice voice. Soft."

Wayne hangs the phone up gently. He feels like he might cry. It comes over him at certain times. He hardly has any control over it. But it is meaningless. Wanda is dead. The woman in Michigan he just called is alive. Her life sounds sordid, sad and lonely. But hopeful too. So who will he cry for? For her? For his son, George? Or for himself? Wanda had been able to cry easily. It seemed to cleanse her of pain. Wayne needs a reason. A rational explanation. Otherwise he feels guilty and self-indulgent. But now the urge seems to have passed. He takes a bottle of whisky out of the drawer of the bedside table and pours himself a large drink. Without water it almost makes him gag. He sips it slowly. He has nothing to cry for. His house is filled with people. Gloria, his daughter, sleeping in George's room, her pregnant girth filling the lower bunk. And downstairs in the spare bedroom his father coughing softly and slowly dying. All he needs to complete this family scene is for his first wife, Gloria's mother, to appear. He smiles, switches off the light and in the darkness is immediately seized by a series of images. It is Wanda. She is dancing. Blond hair lifting from her shoulders and covering her face as she swirls. And then she is running. Across the street in the park. She waves and turns her face toward him as if there was a camera. She is grinning, teeth white and perfect. He closes his eyes tightly and feels the tears slip out. He is ashamed. A grown man crying over the past. It is nothing to be proud of. What happened to the tough young man he used to be? He lingers at the edge of consciousness, speculating and wondering about what he has become. And then he drops into sleep.

In the morning George slides into bed beside him. He nudges his father awake.

"Dad," he whispers. "Dad, it's morning."

"Yeah," says Wayne.

"And it's the weekend, so we can do something."

"Terrific."

"I'll take my clothes down and watch cartoons. After, when you get up, are we going to have a shower?"

"Sure we will. Don't wake Gloria up."

"I won't," says the boy as he scrambles out of the bed and glides out of the room. He stops at the door and turns a serious face to his father, who barely has his eyes open. "Were you drinking a lot last night, Dad?"

Guilt punctures into Wayne's sleepiness. The boy is scared of Wayne's drinking. Shortly after Wanda's death he began to drink constantly. For days he would wander the house in a stupor, leaving pots on the stove to burn, cigarettes in ashtrays to fall out and scar table-tops. The boy was on constant watch for potential danger. He missed school and lived on cereal and milk while he watched over his father, who wept and drank whisky as if it were a balm for his wound. But all that was over. Wayne had control now. He had regained it quickly and held firmly to it, but still he was alert to the boy's fear.

"No, George," he says. "I just had a bit to help me sleep."

"Oh. Well, there's a glass of it beside your bed. It stinks."

"I'll throw it out," Wayne says.

"Okay Dad. See you downstairs."

The boy leaves and Wayne gets up. He dumps the whisky and rinses out the glass. Then, as is his habit, he makes the bed carefully. He is amused by his need for neatness. Everything in its proper place and a proper place for everything. Something his mother had taught him. A constant refrain from his childhood. But it gives him a sense of order and he likes that. He wonders what rituals he is passing on to George. The boy at six lays out his own clothes at night for the next day. Dirty clothes are put in the hamper. If he wakes up to a wet bed the sheet is stripped and the mattress with its rubber cover left to air. Is it right that a little boy should be so self-sufficient? Wayne isn't sure. There is a song that parades through his mind. A constant marching refrain. A few lines really. Felliciano sings it. "I should have loved you better. I didn't mean to be unkind. That was the last thing on my mind . . . ." Wayne guesses the song has more to do with Wanda than with George. Surely it was too early for him to be regretting what he should or could have done for George and hadn't. He picks up his own neatly laid-out clothes and goes downstairs.

Sitting at the dining-room table is his father, Thomas

31

Maitland, aged 68. Diagnosis: cancer of the pancreas. Prognosis: death. He sits drinking coffee and smoking what is probably his tenth cigarette of the day.

"The master has risen," he says loudly.

"Morning, Dad," Wayne says. "How you feeling?"

"Horny, if ya gotta know. I woke up with a hard-on."

"Jeezus, Dad, do you have to talk like that?"

"Am I offending you? I thought that people who made movies all talked dirty."

"I don't make them. I mostly teach other people how to write them."

"Well, the couple that I saw you wrote had pretty steamy language."

"True."

"And nude women."

"Also true. I confess. I write pornography."

"Sit down and I'll pour you coffee," his father says.

"Time for a shower yet?" George calls from the next room.

"Just a few minutes," Wayne shouts back. God, how he hates all this loudness before he's awake. His father's booming voice. George yelling. He yearns for quiet. Or softly played music.

"Here you go," says his father, placing a mug of coffee in front of him.

"I should have my shower with George," Wayne says.

"He's okay for a minute. I never get a chance to talk to you."

This is true. Wayne avoids his father. He is fearful that the old man may feel a need to unburden himself of things that Wayne knows nothing of. Things he doesn't want to know about.

"It's been two weeks now," his father says. "I was just wondering how you felt about me staying here. Things from

32

my end are hunky-dory. But any time you want me to go, just give me the word. I can get a room."

"Everything's okay," Wayne says. "It's working out fine."

"You never had it so good. An old man out doing your shopping. And a daughter slaving over that stove, cooking up a storm. And between the two of us, keeping this place in tip-top shape. I said you had it made. Where is the princess anyway? She still sleeping?"

"Yeah, she is. Listen, Dad, I'm grateful for your help. I worry sometimes you might be overdoing it."

"Don't worry about me. I like to pull my own weight. As long as you're satisfied with that."

"You're holding up your end, Dad."

"That's fine then. So what're you up to today?"

"I'm going to see the plane. They're doing an engine overhaul."

"Taking George?"

"Yeah, I thought I would. Did you tell him you were going to do something with him?"

"No, sir," says Thomas Maitland. "Today I'm just gonna lounge. Read the paper and this aft I may go to the Legion to hoist a few. If I don't make it home don't send out the rescue crew. It just means I've found a softer place to lay my bones for the night. Soft and saucy, I hope." And he laughs loudly at his own joke.

Wayne feels uncomfortable with the conversation. Perhaps it is too close to his own churning lust. He drains his coffee and gets up.

"Good luck with it," he says.

"Well, thanks sonny," his father says.

"Shower time, George!" Wayne calls.

"We should have more talks like this," Thomas Maitland says.

Wayne turns and smiles at the old man, who is looking

serious.

"We will, Dad," he says.

After a shower and a quick breakfast Wayne and George leave the house for the airport. Wayne is anxious to see the plane. His Piper Warrior. Cruising speed, 150 miles an hour. It doesn't fly so much as flash through the sky. He has just moved it from the island airport to a smaller landing-strip just east of Toronto. There is less air traffic and the maintenance people seem to have a great regard for the planes they service. It's cheaper too and this helps allevi-ate some of the guilt that Wayne feels about owning such an extravagance.

It is late March. The weather is windy but mild. The piles of grey slush by the roadside are quickly melting into big pools of water. Although it is still early Saturday morning, the parkway is jammed. Perhaps people are trying to get in one last weekend of skiing, Wayne speculates. He tries to keep a safe distance between his car and the one in front, but other cars keep cutting into the gap. The rhythm of travel is jerky, with lots of stop-and-go. The car in front of Wayne is riding the bumper of the car in front of it. There is a sudden stop and the car in front goes into a skid. He stops by banging into the next car. The owner of this vehi-cle leaps from his car and screams at the other driver. He is so loud that George stops fiddling with the radio.

"That man's real mad," he says.

"This kind of traffic makes you edgy," Wayne says.

The man has stopped screaming and gone back to his car. He opens the back door and takes something from the rear seat and then heads back toward the car that hit him.

"What's he got?" George asks.

"Jeezus, it's a golf club. Looks like a No. 5 iron."

The man swings the club at the windshield of the other car. He hits it several times. Wayne can see the cracks and

34

then the window buckles and begins to fall into the car. The man runs to the side of the car and starts to work on the driver's window. A man and woman scramble out of the passenger door. They stand there silently as the man works his way around the car. Wayne has an urge to try and stop the man, but why? The insurance will pay for it and the man is obviously in a rage. Attempting to interfere might bring a heavy blow to the head. Besides, there is something crazy but comic in his actions. Wayne almost admires him. In less than a minute the man is finished. All the windows are smashed. Traffic is moving again. The man walks calmly back to his car, puts the club in the back seat and then drives away. Wayne pulls out into the stream of moving cars and leaves the bewildered couple standing there alone. Broken and abandoned is the phrase that comes to his mind. He wonders if they even got the other car's licence number. He doubts it. He laughs loudly.

"That guy's bonkers!" he says

"Will that man get in trouble?" George asks.

"Maybe, but one thing's for sure, those people in the other car will never tail-gate again."

"What's tail-gate?" George asks.

"That's when you drive too close behind another car."

"Oh," says the boy. "That guy sure was mad."

Wayne gives another short laugh. They are moving on swiftly now. Whatever was slowing the traffic has been removed. And suddenly he remembers something. He thought he had erased the incident from his mind, but it intrudes now and he lets the flickering images rerun themselves.

It was over a month ago. He was desperate. The need to touch a woman was extraordinary.

He arranged for a neighbour to watch George and went downtown to a small restaurant he knew of where the hookers were still young and soft. He sat in a booth facing

35

the door and drank coffee. It was still early in the day for any action, but he hoped to meet someone who was fresh and eager about the new day. Enthusiastic even. And clean.

He ordered some lunch and halfway through it the parade began. Four young women took the booth across from him. They talked with animation about clothes, how to get salt off their leather boots—mink oil seemed to be the answer—and how so and so was making out in a straight job. Every few seconds one of them would glance over at Wayne and smile. He smiled back. Seated behind the women in another booth were two young men. Watery-eyed and weary looking, Wayne assumed they were pimps. He wondered at their lack of energy. They ignored the women and whispered fiercely back and forth to each other. Wayne thought they might as well have jobs in a mattress factory for all the fun they were having.

The only other customers in the restaurant are several old people, two men and a woman. They are all sitting by themselves and each of them is eating a bowl of soup. Their presence makes Wayne feel sad and he realizes he must leave soon before he becomes maudlin about the fate of old people. Really his own fate.

Because he is the only potential customer all four women are staring at Wayne. He stares back. The women laugh loudly and go into a huddle. Finally one of them slides out from the booth and saunters over to him.

"Want some company?" she says.

"Sure."

She sits down, her tongue licking her lips delicately. There is something prim about her. The pleated skirt and frilly blouse reminding Wayne of school uniforms he has seen young girls wearing. She is slim, youthful and wears little makeup. She is perfect except for her age.

"How old are you?" Wayne asks.

36

"Twenty," she says and smiles. "Ya like this get-up? The old guys really get off on it."

"You look like a schoolgirl."

"That's the whole idea. You wanna party? Sixty bucks for the afternoon. I've got a place too."

"Fifty," Wayne says, "and I'll pay for a motel."

"You got the money?"

He shows her a small wad of bills, turns over three twenties and she nods as she counts with her eyes.

"Okay then," she says. "But before we go ya gotta tell me what place we're gonna be. Ya know, so I can tell somebody. Just kind of like a precaution."

"The Hillcrest Motel on the lakeshore," Wayne says.

"The Hillcrest. I'll tell my friend." She gets up, but before she moves away she turns to Wayne again. "I don't go in for the rough stuff. Nothing off the wall. Just straight."

"Fine," Wayne says.

"I just wanted ya to know. Some guys have got weird ideas."

"Not me."

She goes over to the other women and speaks to them. One of them takes a paper and pencil from her purse and writes down the name of the motel. They are not laughing now. This is business. She comes back to Wayne.

"Ready?" she says.

"Ready."

"My name's Fran," she says.

"Wayne."

He gets up and they leave.

The motel room has two double beds, a colour television and a small bathroom. Fran is in the washroom. The water is running furiously. It makes Wayne want to pee. He hopes she hurries.

"You having a bath?" he yells.

37

"Just cleaning up," she calls back. "You gonna come in and wash yourself?"

"As soon as you come out."

The door opens.

"All yours," she says.

He goes to the toilet, washes his hands and stares at his reflection in the mirror. What am I doing here, he wonders. He feels tense and knows he will be unable to perform sexually. He needs affection, patience. Not things you can buy. But Fran is young. Perhaps she too has a need for a gentle touch. Maybe a moment of tenderness might emerge.

She is sprawled on one of the beds, rummaging through her purse. She puls out a crumpled, hand-rolled cigarette. She lights it and inhales deeply. Wayne is sitting on the other bed. She offers the cigarette to him.

"Wanna toke?" she asks.

"Don't use the stuff," he says.

"A juicer, eh? Most of my tricks are juicers. This stuff'll relax ya without screwing you up."

"I'm fine," he says.

"Listen, take some clothes off, will ya? It always makes me nervous when a guy keeps his clothes on. I figure he's gonna do something. Not normal, ya know."

Wayne smiles and begins to unbutton his shirt. She's as nervous as he is. This makes him feel more at ease. He watches as she takes several more drags of the joint and then butts it. And suddenly he thinks of Gloria. She has placed herself in his care and in a short time the baby will emerge from within her. And there will be two of them. A fist of panic punches him into action. He moves swiftly toward the woman, leans awkwardly over her and places his mouth passionately over hers. She squirms away.

"Look, sorry, mister. Wayne. I don't kiss tricks. I mean, I'll do what you want but I don't do that kind of stuff."

Wayne begins to laugh. The situation is ludicrous. Probably if he wanted her to hang naked from the light fixture while he tickled her toes, that would be acceptable. But no foreplay, please. No kissing or hugging. Has it always been this way? The last prostitute he was with was over twenty years ago. He tries to remember, but it's a blur. He was a kid himself in those days with only one goal in mind. Probably it was the same.

There is a loud banging on the door. The woman tries to get off the bed. Wayne grabs her arm and squeezes it.

"Stay," he says softly. She begins to cry and Wayne buttons up his shirt. A fury is building in him. Something is wrong here. The pounding continues and someone is shouting to open up. The woman opens her mouth to shout and Wayne clamps his hand over her face. He puts his fingers to his lips to warn her. He sees the fear in her eyes. Confident she will be quiet, he goes to the door, waits for the knocking to begin another cycle and when it does he swings it open. The man almost falls into the room. Wayne recognizes him from the restaurant. He has a knife in one hand. Wayne slams the door shut with such force that the man is knocked outside except for the hand holding the knife, which is crushed against the frame. The knife is dropped as the man screams with pain. And then Wayne opens the door again and hauls him inside. He kicks the man hard in the crotch and he goes down, moaning.

The woman on the bed is sobbing.

"Ya came too soon, Charlie. The guy's still got his pants on."

The man tries to get up and Wayne goes to his knees and punches him in the face until blood starts running from his mouth. He gets up and feels weak with disgust. For them and for himself. He retrieves his coat from the bed. The woman stares at him fearfully.

"What am I gonna do with him, mister? You hurt him bad. And I haven't even got cab fare outta here."

He puts his face close to hers and when he speaks it's almost a hiss.

"You're right not to kiss tricks, Fran. You might catch something."

He laughs and hears himself. There is no mirth or joy in this laughter. It is the laugh of a crazy person. And perhaps for the moment he is insane, but as he steps over the groaning body of the young man he has a feeling of release. The tension is drained from him. He feels tired but relaxed. Almost as if he had spent the whole afternnon making love.

It had been a horrible experience. One that he wanted to forget completely, but it came back to re-run itself at the strangest times. Perhaps it was a warning.

"Dad, are we almost there?" George asks.

"Almost," Wayne says. He wonders if he should phone home and check on Gloria. She'll be okay, he assures himself. She's only ten minutes from the hospital by cab. She just has to call her doctor, get a taxi, grab the bag that's been packed for weeks and . . . What? She'll be fine. She managed to conceive this baby without his advice or presence. She's an independent kid. But still, he doesn't like the idea of her being alone. She might be scared.

They reach the small airport and Wayne parks the car and he and George walk toward one of the hangars. The sun is bright and the wind has become a light breeze. A perfect day for flying. Spring hovers on the brink of birth.

"When I grow up I'm going to learn how to fly an airplane too. Aren't I, Dad?"

"If you want," Wayne says.

"Will you teach me?" the boy asks.

Wayne scoops him up and lifts him high in the air and begins to run. The boy holds his arms out as if they were the

40

wings of a plane.

"Wheee," George shouts. "I'm an airplane."

And Wayne runs faster, his breath becoming a gasp. George is flapping his arms now and it is becoming harder for Wayne to keep his balance. He slips on a patch of ice and falls heavily. George lands on top of him.

"Crash landing," the boy shouts.

Wayne lies there for a moment and then, feeling the wet ground seep through the material of his pants, he gets up slowly. He's too old for this, he thinks.

"You okay, Dad?" the boy asks.

"Hunky-dory," he says.

George laughs.

"That's what Grandpa always says."

"I guess I learned it from him."

"And are you going to show me how to fly when I grow up?" George asks.

"Sure I will," Wayne says, but he wonders if the boy will remember to ask him again. At the right time. And he thinks of an old Beatles' song: will you still love me, will you still need me when I'm 64?

Inside the hangar they find the mechanic sitting on his workbench reading the maintenance log. The plane, bright yellow with the name *Wandering Wanda* stencilled across the manifold, is beside him. At moments like this the name, so prominently displayed, embarrasses Wayne, but flying alone at 3000 feet he sometimes fantasizes that heaven really is above and that Wanda can see him and the plane. And perhaps she even laughs with pleasure.

The motor is suspended in a block and tackle a few feet away. The propeller is spread out on the workbench, completely disassembled.

"Needs the works," the mechanic says. "Valves, rings, oil seals. Your prop's got a hairline crack. I'll check it on the

41

machine, but you might have to replace it."

"That's okay," Wayne says. "When will it be ready?"

"Soon as you sign the authorization I'll get crackin' on it," the mechanic says. "Should be ready for next weekend."

"Can we fly then?" George asks.

"Like an eagle," the mechanic says.

"Like an eagle!" says George.

"Sure. The engine'll be so quiet you'll feel like a bird up there."

George laughs.

"Birds don't have motors," he says.

The mechanic gets off the bench and squats to George's height, then looks around furtively as if he is making sure no-one can overhear.

"Says who?" he whispers.

"This guy is crazy," George says. "He thinks birds have motors."

Wayne smiles as he signs the work order. He likes this young man. There is a kind of generosity about him. Wayne feels confident about the work he will do. He wishes he could be more generous. Not about money or things that he has to share but with himself. Often he has the sense of holding back. Waiting for something.

"If you run into complications you'll call me," Wayne says.

"Sure," the mechanic says. "But this one's no real sweat. You've kept it up good."

"See you next week then."

George is still giggling as they leave.

On the highway back to Toronto Wayne has an idea. There is a small lake nearby. A place where he and Wanda used to picnic. At this time of year it will be desolate, but the urge to retrace his steps pulls at him strongly. He turns off on a side road.

"Where are we going?" George asks.

"There's a lake down here," Wayne says. "I'd just like to visit it for a minute."

"Did you use to come here with Mummy?"

"Yeah. A long time ago."

"Is it going to make you sad?" George asks.

"It might," he answers, "but it's okay sometimes to be sad."

"I don't like to be sad," the boy says softly.

It is a small lake, about a mile in length and perhaps half a mile across. Wayne parks carefully. The ground is soft, turning to mud and he doesn't want to get stuck. He stands on the bank and looks out across the water. The cottages along the shoreline are boarded up. The barren trees look starved. It is like a place of bones. No memories stir in Wayne. It's the wrong season.

"Look at that, Dad!" George shouts. "Somebody's swimming."

Wayne sees a small motor-boat with two men slowly making its way across the lake. In the water about ten feet from the boat someone is swimming. A shiver cuts through Wayne. The water must be freezing. A person would have to be crazy to go in the water on a day like this. But he is fascinated. One of the men in the boat is standing up and seems to be shouting at the swimmer. A slight wind has developed and is beginning to make the water choppy, but the swimmer hardly notices. An arm appears for a second and then digs in, pulling the body along. The other arm emerges, dips, pulls. The legs are in constant motion but there is very little splash. The lower half of the swimmer's body operates like the tail of a fish. Propelling and guiding. Excitement bubbles in Wayne. There is something wonderfuly brave about this person. There is no audience clapping or cheering the swimmer on. No crowd shouting its approval. Wayne knows himself to be an exhibitionist. He can perform with great energy in a classroom. At parties he can be entertaining. Often people think he is hilarious and he receives many invitations to speak at banquets and even at political functions. Often he responds and his success always surprises him because alone he is frightened. Even in the plane he knows fear more than anything. The swimmer appears fearless and uncaring about whether or not anyone is watching.

Wayne takes George's hand in his own.

"Come on," he says. "Let's go down and meet them."

The boy and his father scramble down the bank and run along the beach. The swimmer is only a few yards from the shore and has pulled ahead of the boat.

"Pull! Pull!" the man standing in the boat yells.

Finally the water is too shallow and the swimmer stands up. Wayne is astonished. Even before she takes off the cap of the wet-suit he can see the swimmer is a woman. A very young woman. He laughs.

"What's so funny?" she says.

"I was watching. We were, and I just assumed you were a guy."

She comes out of the water and sits on an old log.

"Gotta catch my breath," she says.

"Aren't you freezing?" George asks.

She grins at the boy and a pair of lovely dimples crease her face. A desire to run pushes at Wayne.

"Naw," she says. "This suit keeps me pretty warm."

The boat pulls up and the man doing all the shouting jumps out.

"How ya feeling, Berny?" he says.

"My name's Bernice," she says, holding out her hand to Wayne. He takes it and then feeling the coldness covers it with his other hand.

"I'm Wayne," he says. "Wayne Maitland. This is my son, George."

"Hi, George," she says. "Your dad's got nice warm hands."

George looks away shyly. Wayne is embarrassed and lets go of her hand.

"This is my coach, Al Dunitz," she says. "The guy in the the boat's Pete."

Wayne shakes hands with Al and nods at the other man.

"Nice to meet you," Al says. He's in his fifties and he's wearing a heavy windbreaker and a baseball cap, with a whistle looped around his neck. An aging jock, Wayne thinks.

"How come you gotta coach?" George asks.

"'Cause I'm gonna swim the lake," Bernice says.

"This lake?" George says.

"No. THE lake. Lake Ontario," she says.

The boy looks puzzled.

"All of it?" he says.

She laughs. "All of it," she answers.

"Let's get you back to the van so you can change, Berny," Al says.

"You live in the city, Wayne?" she asks.

"Yeah, we do," Wayne says.

"Can I grab a ride back with you?"

"Don't pull this on me, Berny. I wanna talk with you."

"If I go with him," she says, "I'll get a lecture. Throw me my bag, Pete." The man in the boat tosses out a flight bag, which she catches. "I'll go change up in the trees. I'll just be a jiff."

"Berny, you'll catch a cold!" But she's gone. Al fiddles with his whistle for a few seconds. "Look," he says. "Wayne. Don't get the wrong idea here. I just worry about her. She's only eighteen."

"I don't want to interfere," Wayne says.

**45**

"She's always pulling stunts like this. Eats junk food, smokes grass. Swimming Lake Ontario is a serious business. She can do it but she needs more discipline . . . . You got any ID with ya?"

Wayne takes out his wallet and shows his driver's licence. Al studies it and flips through the credit cards.

"Sorry," he says, handing it back. "I feel responsible to her parents. But they can't control her either. She can go with you. Probably talk your ear off. She's a good kid."

Bernice appears at the top of the bank. She is dressed in slacks, a long quilted coat and a brilliant red toque.

"Ready," she says.

"You be at the pool 10 sharp tomorrow morning," Al says.

"Okay Al. See you, Pete." She waves at them and begins to walk away. George and Wayne have to run to catch up.

"Do you swim here a lot?" Wayne asks when he comes alongside of her.

"This is the first time. Al doesn't approve, but with the wet-suit I'm well insulated. I like the open water."

"I know that feeling," he says.

"You a swimmer?"

"No, I fly a plane."

"Dad's got his own plane," George says. "It's his and mine. And when I'm bigger, he's gonna teach me to be the pilot."

"That's wonderful," she says. "Then you can take me for a ride."

"We could take you sooner than that. Couldn't we, Dad?"

"It's a possibility," Wayne says. He suddenly thinks the world is full of possibilities. He smiles as he imagines his father sitting in the Legion, drinking beer and trying to seduce some old doll who's giggling and acting coy. And

46

probably Gloria is soaking in a warm bath, her hands caressing the hump of her stomach. She is dreaming of the baby who will soon be in her arms. And she is scared, excited and almost confident.

At the car Bernice and George have a small argument about the seating arrangements.

"I always sit by the window," George says. "You sit in the middle."

"I like the window too," she says.

"I'll get sick," George says.

"How about if you sit on my lap?" she says.

"Okay," says George.

Wayne feels an unusual contentment as he starts the car. It may be late in the game but there are still possibilities.

## Stretch Marks

It started with the pigeons. They had built a nest on the ledge outside the bathroom window. It was constructed of small twigs held together with mud. Gloria watched the two birds build the crude thing. She observed them daily and was filled with mixed emotions. No, that sounded like the name of a rock-and-roll band. What she felt was disgust at how dirty they were. Because they were big birds, their droppings were large and, from the eavestrough down, one whole side of the house was stained. Even the nest itself was encrusted with white deposits. There was nothing dainty about the pigeons, Gloria concluded. Sometimes though, while she watched, a strand of sadness, like a hair caught in the throat, would choke her. Their awkwardness made her cry. They did not fly in the fluid way other birds did. They flapped their wings furiously and wobbled into space. Only occasionally when they were well airborne did they glide easily and appear graceful. When the two eggs appeared in the nest she studied them more closely. The male was grey-blue in colour. He had a long neck, on which a small head constantly swivelled. Gloria decided he was a first-time father, unsure of himself and nervous. Maybe, she thought, he wasn't prepared for this new role. The black markings along each wing were like racing stripes. If he had been born with shoulders he might have been a football player. And she would imagine herself knitting a tiny little sweater with No. 9 on it, her favourite number, and finding somewhere a set of miniature shoulder-pads for him to wear. In her mind she could see him strutting along the peak of the roof in this get-up, making signals to other neighbourhood pigeons and being a kind of quarterback of the sky.

The day Gloria cut a hole in the bathroom window-screen and began to push crusts of bread into the nest she also named them. Flo and Frank. Flo of course was the female and she spent most of her time on the nest warming the eggs. Frank foraged for food and guarded the territory. Occasionally he did a stint on the nest and Gloria noticed he was more cautious in his movements around the eggs than Flo. Flo tended to land heavily and flop herself down. She would then squirm around until she got comfortable. All the bouncing and moving around got Gloria nervous. The eggs could be crushed. Frank seemed to be more care-ful. He never landed on the nest but perched beside it and climbed in gingerly. Once he took up a position he never moved.

49

Frank reminded Gloria of her father. Two uneasy creatures, a man and a bird but both males and as such a million miles from her understanding. She sometimes thought that men had established different boundaries and lived their lives at a great distance from women. It was like women were stalked by men, trapped, captured and then put in domestic cages. And then men fled back into whatever wilderness they had created for themselves. Secret places in darkened cave-like rooms echoing with muffled voices and clinking glasses. Did they hide because they felt guilty about the enormity of the tasks they had left their women to cope with? Were they uncomfortable with the thought of dirty floors, full ashtrays, crying babies waiting at their homes to accuse them when they finally returned? Did these images haunt them like unfriendly ghosts? Or was it just her father?

She was only eighteen but she knew certain things that no-one would be able to convince her weren't true. She just knew. For instance, she knew that debris, bad smells and dirty dishes didn't bother her. Vacuum-cleaners, air-fresheners and dishwashers were created by and for men. She knew that her father was obsessed with cleanliness and order. Everything in its place. Tidy up after yourself. These were important matters by which he measured your worth. Her father could not stand a mess. She knew that the biggest pile of unwashed laundry would never faze her. She would walk around it while her father put through one load after another, frantic in his need to launder the world and with his washing-machine conquer the gravy stains that seemed to pursue him. Her understanding of him led her to believe that he equated gravy stains with failure. And failure with chaos. The idea of things beyond his control seemed to frighten him. What nonsense, she thought. To think you could have control over anything. Well, maybe what colour toothbrush you preferred. Things like that. Things that didn't really matter. But the big stuff, like who you were going to fall in love with, was unpredictable. When you were born and when you died could not be controlled. She knew that for sure. But the space between birth and death should be filled with loving. Between eating, sleeping, working and all the other activities that kept people busy there needed to be loving. That seemed to be true but she wasn't sure. What was love anyway but a kind of consoling?

Gloria looks out of the bathroom window on this May morning. The sun is high already and hot. She has slept late. This last month she has been tired all the time. The baby has dropped and sits precariously balanced in her pelvic zone like a bowl of jellied salad that she fears will spill from its container and end up on the floor in a pile of multi-coloured chunks. The baby inside her is sort of like a dress pattern. She knows what it should look like but she is unsure of her ability to make it turn out the right shape. She is afraid. It is a faceless fear, like the boy in that darkened room almost nine months ago, when after too many beers she had allowed herself to be led away from the music and had succumbed to him in a brief sexual skirmish. When she thought of the child growing inside her she remembered that boy with a sense of longing. The longing was not for the boy but rather a long wailing wish that she could have known who he really was and that she could have liked him. She wonders again what price must be paid for that mistake. What penalty can she afford beyond imagining her baby with the face of an eggshell, no mouth, no nose or eyes. Just a smooth surface waiting for her to etch in the features. And in her imagination she could not. This was her punishment. Or was it? Maybe all new mothers suffered this sense of mystery.

51

Gloria looks out the window and her eyes focus on the nest. It is empty except for the two eggs. And then she sees that one of them has been squashed. The shell is shattered and pushed in. But no liquid has seeped out, she thinks in a panic. It's just a dent. The baby pigeon inside is probably fine. But where are Flo and Frank? She scans the area and has to climb awkwardly up on the toilet to get a better view. She spots them on the roof of a building several houses over. Flo, looking pretty and serene, with her soft grey feathers resting smoothly and with a slight ruffle of mauve at her throat, is clucking gently and seems to stare off into the cloudless sky. Frank is circling overhead, his flight path fashioned into short, tight patterns. He looks like a running back searching the air for a pass that will never come. He touches down on various roofs and signals loudly to Flo, but she ignores him. Gloria senses that some kind of process of selection is going on. Will they mate again, she wonders, and start over? Is it too late? And if it is, what will hold them together? Can pigeons be tender to one another in the midst of tragedy? Can they console each other?

She feels the heat of anger building in her body. All the stupid things had to do was come home. She would still push bread crusts through the hole in the screen. They wouldn't starve. And maybe the one egg would hatch and they could complete their duties as parents. But not if they abandoned the nest. She had come home. Home to a father she hardly knew. Home to a father locked into an inconsolable grief for his recently-dead wife. It hadn't been easy for her to come here after her own mother had booted her out, calling her a slut, but she had learned to live with the ghost of what she supposed would be called her stepmother and a very alive seven-year-old half-brother and a grandfather she had not even met up until a month ago who himself was dying of cancer. She had adapted to the situation, adjusted to the distance her father kept, the jealousy of the boy and the bad jokes of the old man. She wanted her child to have a home. This was the best she could do for now. Later she might do better.

Gloria watches the pigeons for a long time. Frank is sitting for longer periods of time at each new location as if he can mobilize Flo with a demonstration of calm patience. And suddenly she does take flight and glides in ever narrowing circles around the roof peak where Frank is perched and waiting. And then she lands. It is a house almost half a block away and Gloria cannot see them clearly. They appear to be just sitting, each facing in a different direction. Gloria is feeling stiff and tired from all the straining. She is about to give up when she sees Frank swoop down toward the ground. He reappears in a moment and Gloria can see there is something dangling from his beak. A piece of string perhaps, but whatever it is she knows a decision has been made. They aren't coming back.

She watches a while longer. Flo is helping Frank now and they are obviously rebuilding. A few days from now there will be a new nest. And then another batch of eggs. The cycle has begun again. Gloria admires how easily the two birds can start over. But she hates them for it too. What about the egg left behind? How can they be so unfeeling? Don't birds believe in history?

She climbs down from her perch, goes to the bedroom and dresses. George watches from the doorway as she struggles into a cotton shift.

"You sure are fat," he says.

"Doors are for knocking," she says. And she vows again to herself that if she has a boy he will learn at an early age to respect other peoples' privacy. Girls aren't nearly the trouble boys are. Her mother told her that.

"And for opening and closing," George says.

"So close it and leave."

"Did you make up your mind to keep it yet?" he asks.

"What?" she says and wonders if all seven-year-olds are like George. God, they could drive you nuts. That was reason enough right there to give the kid up.

"If you're going to keep the baby after it's born."

"I don't know," she says honestly.

"Dad says they're a lot of work. But I could help you. If he's a boy I could take him in my bath."

"What if it's a girl?"

"That would be okay. She could still come in my bath until she got too old. You know."

She crosses the room and pulls the boy tight against her belly. There is a swirling of emotions inside her, like a whirlpool sucking her into a bottomless lake of sadness. Tears dribble down her cheeks and she begins to shake with rage at this overwhelming sense of uncertainty. Damn it, here she was living in a whole houseful of men and the only one who offered any help was a seven-year-old. Good old Dad was his usual secretive self, never offering his opinion, advice or anything. Well, he did let her stay and he had never mentioned when she had to go. But she knew if she kept the child she wouldn't be welcome. And then there was Grandpa, his prostate removed and the cancer still gnawing at him like a horde of moths devouring an old woolen blanket. Waiting for death with what she thought was a weird sense of humour. He only let the doctors renew his prescriptions for a week at a time, said he didn't plan to leave an estate made up of pills and potions. How would he feel about a new life with all the sounds and smells it would bring dominating his last days? She could imagine the infant sitting on the old man's lap and peeing on him and he would laugh and start to choke like he did and then something would break inside him and he would fall on the floor,

54

the baby squashed under his dead body. Of course. And in this scene she saw her father suffering on the sidelines, his head nodding as if he had expected the worst all along.

"You're squishing me," George says.

"Oh, sorry," she says and releases him.

"You daydream a lot," he says.

"I guess I do."

"What were you thinking about?" he asks.

She laughs.

"You're just like my father, always trying to get inside my head."

"My dad too."

"Our father," she says. "Anyway, I was thinking it's too bad you're my brother and you're only seven."

"How come?"

"So you could marry me and take me away from all this."

"That's cookoo," he says.

She laughs again.

"I'll settle for a cup of tea," she says.

"It's almost lunch."

Why is it, she wonders, that little kids end up keeping track of things like that? It's like they're born with some moral code about what is right and wrong and they have been assigned the task of keeping score. Probably she was like that too. When she was young. Or still?

The two of them go downstairs and march into the kitchen, arm in arm. The old man is sitting at the table drinking tea, his own private teapot in front of him. The other person at the table she suspects is her father, but all she can see is a pair of hands holding an open newspaper. Are they his hands? Up until very recently the hands could have belonged to one of the women her grandfather brought home from the Legion and sat up all night with, drinking beer and playing strange music. Some guy named John Pratt singing, You'll get used to it, over and over again. It was pretty awful and finally her father made a new rule: no overnight guests. So more than likely the hands were his.

"I have an announcement to make," she says.

The newspaper is lowered and the questioning face of Wayne Maitland, script-writer, teacher and father, is revealed. Her grandfather grins in anticipation. She loves the way he expects your best. Her father's face is set grimly, waiting for the worst.

"Pigeons," she says loudly, "are for the birds."

There is a strained silence. The old man rolls a cigarette, a tolerant smile on his face. Her father wears a frown but his features are still soft. There is a willingness to accept whatever new burden she has dreamed up. The face of her father is sad and later in the day it will harden into anger.

"Is that a joke or a puzzle?" he asks.

"I've decided to get married," she says.

"Who to?" he asks.

"I haven't decided yet."

She pours a cup of coffee for herself and takes a chair at the table. George tries to sit on her lap but slides off her knees.

"After you have the baby you get your lap back, right?"

"Right."

"And I get to be an uncle. Right?"

"That's right. The youngest uncle in the world."

"Will I really be the youngest uncle?"

She smiles at the boy. Where did this idea come from? Is it just another way to pick a fight with her father or is she going to act? One of his favourite expressions was, If you lay track make sure you know where it's going because sooner or later a trainload of people will come along. It was his way of telling her to be responsible. Well, she was. Totally. And would be.

56

"Will I be the youngest uncle?" George asks again.

"Yes," she says, "and when I get married you'll have an uncle."

"Good," the boy says. "Good. Good. And will he come and live with us?"

Her father groans.

"If you don't have a certain person picked," her grandfather says, "I could introduce you to a couple of guys down at the Legion. Some of them could do with a little taking care of."

Gloria struggles to her feet.

"Now hear this, you guys! I don't want a man I have to take care of. And I don't want a man who feels he's stuck with taking care of me. The man I'm going to marry will be . . ." She stops, unsure of how to describe this person of her dreams.

"What, a saint?" her father says.

"A nest-builder," she says.

"Listen, Gloria," he says. "You've got to snap out of this dream world. You've got to face up to reality and make some decisions.."

"Don't fuss at her, Wayne," the old man says.

"You stay out of this, Dad. You're just as bad. Worse. You should be resting, taking care of yourself and instead you're playing senior-citizen Casanova. Sometimes I think you can't wait to die."

"My hurry is to live, son. I'm in no rush to die."

"You aren't going to die, are you, Grandpa?" George asks. He walks over to the old man and takes his hand. Thomas Maitland takes it and squeezes it.

"Not for some time," he says.

"I hope I never get cancer," the boy says in a frightened voice. "First it killed my mum and now it wants to take you away."

"Jesus Murphy!" Wayne shouts, hitting the table and rising from his chair. And then more softly, "Jeezus. I'm sorry." He sits down again.

Thomas Maitland has George in his arms now. The boy is crying quietly.

"I guess I opened up a can of worms," Gloria says. "You'd think I would have learned to keep my mouth shut."

"No harm done," the old man says. "We're a family."

"So what about the baby?" Wayne asks.

"I'm going to keep it," Gloria says.

"Hey, hey, that's terrific news," Thomas Maitland says.

"What?" says George, wiping the tears from his eyes.

"Your sister is going to keep the baby!"

"So then I will be an uncle," George says.

"How and where?" Wayne asks.

"Somewhere, somehow," she answers brightly.

Wayne sighs and gets up again.

"I have a script waiting to be born," he says.

"Is this the one about the giant pickerel in Lake Ontario that eats the CN Tower and destroys Toronto?" the old man asks, his face serious.

Gloria laughs and George snorts indignantly.

"My dad doesn't write stupid movies like that," he says.

Wayne is amused and allows a small smile to appear for a moment.

"Most of what your father writes never gets to be a movie, period. This is just a treatment I'm doing for a producer. It's about these six couples who board a train in Halifax. They all know each other and they plan to ride all the way out to Vancouver because train service is going to be stopped completely and this is their last chance. Anyway," he says, getting excited by the plot, "someone or something starts to kill them off shortly after they get started. One by one. And then the train staff disappear but the train keeps going.

58

Soon it's down to one couple. They want to get off but the train is out of control. It just hurtles through Montreal, on to Toronto and on and on. Like that."

"So what happens, Dad?" George asks.

"They die of boredom in Sudbury," Thomas Maitland says.

"I don't know yet," Wayne says. "I've got to figure out a way for them to escape but it can't be easy."

"Superman could save them," George says. "A super hero could."

"Or maybe," Thomas Maitland says, "there's another train coming from Vancouver. Another mystery train with people being knocked off and just one couple left. And the two trains crash, get derailed and one person from each of the couples gets killed but then the survivors climb out of the wreckage, see each other and fall madly in love. It could be kind of a love story."

Laughing loudly, Gloria says, "What happens if the two survivors are both guys?"

"Probably do a roaring business," the old man says.

"You've all been a great help," Wayne says. "With your inspiration bubbling in my brain I should be able to finish this thing today. What are other people doing?"

"I'm going to the movies," George says. "Can I, Dad? I got my own money."

"Sure, but come home after the matinée. No staying to see it twice."

"Okay," the boy says and he gets up to leave.

"Just about time for me to totter over to the Legion. See what's cooking."

"Go easy on the beer," Wayne says.

"I know. I know," the old man says. "Make sure I eat something and don't leave any crumbs. I'll be fine, Wayne."

"Are you going to walk?" his son asks him.

59

"I believe I'm still capable."

"Well, make sure you take a cab home."

The old man is standing and grinning at Wayne, but then turns to Gloria.

"Who would have thought it would turn out like this? You know, he phones the Legion when I'm there to make sure I'm okay. Pretty soon I'm going to have to have a note before they let me in the place."

He laughs, rubs Gloria's belly playfully and walks away.

"Good luck with the husband-hunting," he shouts back. "I hear they've got computers now that can match you up with the right person in a minute."

Gloria and Wayne sit quietly for a few seconds. There is a stillness in the house now that the other two have left. A strange weariness begins to overtake Gloria. It's like a sudden fog, heavy and humid, difficult to breathe. She tries to free herself from its weight and then realizes it originates in her father.

"You have a lot of responsibilities with the bunch of us," she says.

"He's a very sick man. The doctors don't know how he keeps going."

"How do you do it?"

"What?"

"Day after day. Getting up every day. Looking after us."

"I have to," he says.

"Don't you ever want to scream at us all to screw off? Leave you alone?"

"Sometimes I feel a little pressed."

"You must miss Wanda but you never show it."

"What's the point?" he asks.

"If we knew, George and me and your dad, maybe we could be better company for you."

"You do fine," he says. "I'm just tired."

"I think you're lonely. Even with the bunch of us around. And you don't even get mad about it."

"I just try to accept things the way they are."

"I'd be pounding the walls. Yelling and screaming."

"I guess that's the difference between us," he says and gets up from the table. "I've got to get to work."

"You know, you sort of act like your life is over," Gloria says.

He stands there for a moment, his face tightening into an expressionless mask. A sudden image takes possession of his imagination. He sees himself in the cockpit of his plane. He sees himself flying, free and easy through the air. But the sky before him is empty and endless. He knows he is going nowhere. It could be a lonely feeling, if he were to let it in.

"Don't worry about me," he says. "Concentrate on your own problems."

"I have to know if you'll let me stay on after the baby's born," she says.

He has anticipated this moment many times and in the previews of the scene that he has watched he chose to be rigid and cruel. He would not bend the shape of his life to accommodate a grandchild. He would use the opportunity to force Gloria into making some realistic decisions. She must understand that she couldn't rely on him for the rest of her life. But what would she do? And what price in guilt would he be asked to pay?

"Why do you say it like that? Of course you and the baby can stay."

"You never mention it. Does the idea of being a grandfather scare you?"

"I don't think about it. Anyway, you hadn't made up your mind about keeping it. There was no point in me deciding until you did."

"Is it really okay with you?" she asks.

He hesitates, wanting to tell her the truth. He would like to tell her of lying in a hot tub of water late at night when she and the others are asleep, and making a pyramid with his hands held over his chest. And then closing his eyes tightly and waiting for the blue dot to form in his darkened vision. He would attempt to move the blue dot inside the pyramid. Patiently he would manoeuvre it between the open walls of his hands. When it was in the middle, he would close his hands, hoping to trap the blue dot inside the pyramid. But it never worked. There were times when he felt his life depended on making it work. How could he explain it?

"We'll cope," he says. "Besides, your magic man may appear at any moment."

"You think I'm silly."

Yes, she is silly, he thinks. And desperate because she lacks the rituals that can create a sense of safety. Catching little blue dots in cupped hands. Nurturing dormant avocado pits into flourishing plants. He wonders how she locates a centre of calm for herself. He wishes he could remember the lullabies he sang to her when she was an infant. He wishes his life were a warm cradle he could rock her safely to sleep in.

"I think," he says, "I should get to work. Do you have a plan for finding this man?"

"No. It's just that ... "

She does not know how to explain the emptiness she feels that the growing child only emphasizes. It is a kind of nameless terror not mentioned in polite company. She feels the child consuming her, taking over her every thought and feeling. After the delivery all that will be left of her is an empty shell. An abandoned husk. And at that very moment of greatest fear she must find the strength to become a mother. On her own.

"Let's take a ride down to the lake," her father says.

"You're supposed to be working."

"By my own order. Right now I'd like the comfort of being near the water."

"I'll get a sweater," she says.

In the car they are silent. It is a short drive to Cherry Beach, but Gloria uses the time to convince herself that her father is going to try and talk her out of keeping the child. She is frightened of the ominous power he is capable of exercising. He could have her committed to a psych ward someplace, get a power of attorney by declaring her incompetent, then when the baby was born it could be taken from her and adopted by parents more suitable. More suitable than her. By the time her father has parked she feels ill with apprehension. He looks over at her and smiles, unaware of her consuming fear.

"Let's walk on the beach," he says.

"All right," she agrees, hoping that co-operation will earn her a reprieve from the lecture she is sure her father is about to deliver.

They walk down to the water and both look out over the wide expanse of Lake Ontario. The wind is calm, which allows the gulls to float easily overhead in their quest for debris that might be edible. There are several small sailing craft gliding smoothly over the water's surface. A large lake freighter looms on the horizon, barely moving as it eases its way along the path to a docking berth.

There is an orderliness in this scene that Wayne finds reassuring. Everything is visual. He can see it all. All activity is on the surface or above it. For the moment he is not interested in the depth of the water. He does not want to think of undercurrents. He understands what he can see and he is filled with a sense of expansiveness as the sun begins to warm his skin.

There are a few other people walking along the shoreline. Old couples, arms linked, heads turned toward the
lake, looking out at the water, sometimes pointing with
their arms or canes at sudden movements that might be
small waves or darting birds. Several young women are
strolling with their children, who dart to the water's edge
and dunk their feet. Their squeals of protest about the freezing water are shrill. The mother yell back at them and promise severe punishment if they do this again to their shoes.
And then the mothers turn back to one another, to their
conversations. And the children, tempted once more, step
into the lake up to their ankles. And all this is watched by
the single grownups, wary, middle-aged city people seeking
solitude, momentary relief perhaps from an office job, a
place to breathe more easily and make that critical decision
that may irrevocably affect the remainder of the life that is
left to them. They come to walk, watch and wait for certain
things to unfold. Perhaps, Wayne thinks, all those who
come here feel crowded in some way. This would explain
how careful everyone is to give plenty of room to the others. Wayne notices that people will sometimes even walk
around the footmarks of those who have gone before them.

"I can't imagine doing something when there is no end
in sight," Wayne says.

"You mean having a baby or raising it?" Gloria asks.

Wayne laughs and takes her arm. They begin to walk
along the beach.

"Neither. I was thinking of Bernice wanting to swim
across the lake."

"She's crazy."

"No more than you."

"I'd like to meet her some time. How come you never
bring her around?"

"I'm embarrassed to."

"Because she's my age?"

"Partly, but mostly I don't know how I feel about her."

"But if you avoid her, then you'll never know. Right?"

"You're pretty smart."

"I learned from you," she says.

Wayne is startled by her remark. He cannot remember ever consciously trying to teach her anything. Most of her life was lived with her mother. He hardly was ever with her. What could she possibly have learned from him?

"I was trying to think," Wayne says, "to remember some things that Wanda told me I could tell you. About having the baby."

"I was thinking of Wanda and you this morning," Gloria says, "when I was talking about getting a husband. You and her always seemed to . . . I don't know. Be there for each other. Like what happened to her was happening to you too. You know what I mean? And that's what I want."

"It's strange," Wayne says. "One time before George was born, Wanda and I had this talk about what she'd do if I died. She had it worked out how she'd take care of the kid. The money details. Everything. The funny thing was we never had a conversation about what would happen if she died."

"I guess neither of you thought it could happen."

"My point is that nothing is perfect. Wanda and I got along pretty good, but we made mistakes, had fights. Didn't talk for days sometimes. So maybe you'll find a husband some time and you'll have a great partnership but there'll be problems. In the meantime, you've got us."

"You, George and Grandpa."

"We're not a bad lot."

"I know," she says softly.

Suddenly she is very tired. This is not what she expected.

She realizes her body has been tensed to argue, to fight for the right to choose. And now here it is, given to her so easily. She feels weary enough to fall. Or weep. She stops and looks at her father.

"There's one other thing I need to know," she says.

"What?"

"Do you really want to be part of this? Are you choosing too?"

"Yes," he answers, and she reaches and hugs him awkwardly.

"Thank you, Daddy," she says and then laughs at his expression. "That's what you are, you know."

He nods solemnly. Perhaps, he thinks, this has always been his difficulty with Gloria, her desire for him to be Daddy and his refusal to accept the role. Maybe he was paying Gloria back for his own suffering. And then he smiles as something Wanda once said comes back to him.

"What're you thinking?" Gloria asks.

"Men don't get stretch marks," he says laughing. "Wanda told me that. It just struck me as being funny. I remember she used to rub baby oil on her stomach every night when she was carrying George. But after he was born she still had these faint marks and she said they would never let you forget you were a mother."

"Can we sit down?" Gloria asks.

"Over there," Wayne says, "where that young guy is playing the guitar. I want to ask him something."

There is a young man, wearing an inexpensive suit that he has grown out of, sitting on a wooden bench, strumming a battered-looking guitar. The instrument case is propped up beside him, so he is not panhandling like Wayne had thought he might be. But the young man has a worn, weary look that makes Wayne feel confident about the proposal he is going to make. Still, he feels nervous as he strides up

66

to the young man. He could make a fool of himself.

"Hello," he says.

The young man stops playing and looks past Wayne to Gloria, who is struggling her way to the bench. She heaves herself down with a groan.

"You're carrying quite a load there," the young man says. Wayne holds out his hand.

"My name's Wayne Maitland," he says. "This is my daughter, Gloria."

"Hi there," the young man says, taking Wayne's hand but looking at Gloria. "My name's Gregory."

"I was wondering," Wayne says. "I heard you playing there a minute ago. Do you know any lullabies?"

Gregory laughs, the sound a deep rumble. It is an infectious sound and in a moment Gloria is laughing too. Wayne is determined to wait them out, but something in him is tickled too and he joins them. But he must speak. Explain.

"My daughter," he chokes out, "is going to have a baby."

"I noticed," Gregory says, his eyes crinkled with mirth.

"We don't know any lullabies," Wayne says.

This sobers Gregory. He looks at Gloria, a searching, penetrating gaze. And then at Wayne, who feels stupid and wishes that he had never embarked on the pursuit of this crazy idea.

"That's a serious drawback. But I know plenty of them. I could teach you some."

"What a terrific idea," Gloria says.

"I was thinking you could come to supper some night," Wayne says.

"What about tonight!" Gloria says. "We could all learn. Dad, you could call Grandpa at the Legion. He likes to sing. George would like it."

"Who's George?" Gregory asks.

"My brother," Gloria says.

67

"You got no husband?" Gregory asks.

"No," she says.

"Well, I've got no plans for tonight," he says.

"Come on then, my dad's car's over here."

Gregory puts his guitar in its case and then helps Gloria up. Wayne stands apart and back as the two of them walk toward the car. They are talking rapidly and laughing. He doesn't know what they are saying. He doesn't need to know. He is filled with a sense of wonder that this very night he will learn a lullaby from a stranger and some time not too far off he will hold an infant in his arms that will be his grandchild.

## If Words Could Make Wishes Come True

The boy is deep in sleep, dreaming. There is a woman in the dream, perhaps his mother. The woman is smiling at him and holding his hands as they sit on the ground across from each other. The woman's features are faded, like a memory handled too often. He cannot see her clearly, but her hands are warm to his touch. He feels her smiling eyes looking into his and the river that flows past them just a few feet away makes a gently swishing sound that causes a bubbling sensation in his throat. He hears his own laughter and then the woman begins to rock back and forth, pushing him back and pulling him forward. Finally, he falls into her lap and the woman flips herself over so she is on top, holding him down with her strong arms. The boy struggles to free his pinned shoulders, but he cannot stop laughing long enough to focus his strength. Suddenly she lets go and holds her arms above him in a circle. He sits up and she engulfs him in a tender embrace. He bristles with happiness. He realizes they have not spoken. He wants to tell her something. A secret. Something she will never forget. But then he hears the ringing and she disappears. The sound is coming from a place outside his sleep and in the instant he leaves the dream and comes awake he realizes it is a phone ringing. He opens his eyes to the sunlit room that he recognizes as his own. But on the small table beside his bed is a bright red telephone. Ringing. The presence of the phone puzzles him. When he went to sleep the night before there had been no phone. It continues to ring loudly. He lifts the receiver and holds it to his ear. He hears laughter.

"Hello," he says.

"Happy birthday, George," says a familiar voice.

"Dad?" the boy says.

"Surprised you, didn't I? The phone company installed the plug yesterday. After you were asleep last night, I snuck in and left it so I could call you. Do you like it?"

"I like red," George says.

"Now you can call all your friends whenever you want."

George imagines his father downstairs in the kitchen talking to him on the white wall phone. It makes him feel frightened, as if there is a long distance between them.

"You have your own private number," his father says.

For a second, George remembers the woman in his dream, but he knows she will never call him. She was just a dream.

"Is this my birthday present?" he asks.

"Come down and find out," his father says.

"Okay, Dad. Bye. Thanks." But the line has gone dead. He listens to the dial-tone for a few seconds, and decides that having his own phone is okay. Other kids have video games. One boy even has a computer. But none of them have their own phone. He hangs up the receiver and gets out of bed. On his way to the bathroom he begins to plan who he will call first and who he will give his number to. And he must get a book to keep the names and numbers of his friends, so he can call them anytime he wants. He will get a book, just like his father's.

George's father, Wayne, sits on a stool looking out of the big kitchen window into the back yard. Today his son is eight. He tries to remember what it felt like when he was eight. It is too long ago to recapture. Almost 35 years. But certain events have remained fixed in his memory, like being in Grade 3, which meant, at last, that he was allowed to write out his lessons with pen and ink. No more printing with pencils. He remembered the long wooden pens with the removable nibs. And the ink-wells at each desk. And when he was eight he joined the Cubs even though he hated tying knots. He liked the uniform. Even the short pants. And that was the year he got the paper route. All these things he remembered because, at the time, they made him feel like he was growing up. How desperate he was then to race ahead through the years, to find a time and place when he would be grown up. When he was young, he had believed there would be a point where wishes would no longer be necessary; that everything he had ever dreamed of or longed for would come into being of its own accord. And then, he would know for sure that he was grown up.

He stands as he hears the boy's footsteps coming down the stairs. Hurriedly, he lights the candles on the cake. It is a huge creation, much too big for the two of them, but he is pleased with the effect it makes. The cake is the very best that Laura Secord makes. It is chocolate-filled, with an almond icing. It is decorated with candy space-ships and George's name is written in red icing sugar. Wayne hopes that this cake will let the boy know how special he is.

Wayne looks up and sees George in the hallway. The boy sees the cake, smiles and begins to run. Wayne sings.

"Happy birthday to you. Happy birthday to you. Happy birthday, dear George. Happy birthday to you."

"What a neat cake! But birthday cake in the morning!" George says.

"Why not?" says Wayne. "Blow out the candles before they melt."

The boy obeys and the candles are extinguished with one breath, but then there is an awkward second or two when father and son seem unsure of what to say or do.

"Hey, look out there," Wayne says, pointing to the window.

George looks and sees a new bicycle propped against the fence in the back yard.

"A dirt bike! It looks like an MX."

"Go see. Take it for a spin. I'm gonna make us some cheese omelettes."

He turns from the boy, intent on making breakfast, but George grabs him around the waist in a fierce hug.

"Thank you, Dad."

"See if you even like it first," says Wayne, pulling away from the embrace.

"I mean for the phone too. And everything," the boy says.

"That's okay," Wayne says, his back to the boy, rooting around in the refrigerator, distracting himself with the preparations for breakfast. But when the boy is gone Wayne stations himself at the window to watch. He sees George

72

run his hand along the crossbar of the new bike. A lump comes to his throat as the boy swings into the seat and pedals out of sight down the laneway. Happy and sad feelings bump into each other and jostle for control. He moves back to the counter and grates more cheese for the omelettes. The eggs are already beaten, creamy smooth in a bowl. George loves lots of cheese and Wayne finds the notion of moving his arm back and forth soothing. Comforting even. He is aware of an inner fragility. He does not know its source and he does not want to discover it. Instead, he remembers another bike. He was twelve when he bought it with his own money. Four years he saved for it. It was a Raleigh, a British bike. The best at the time. It was black with gold markings and he was proud of it, but even prouder of himself for not expecting his father to buy it for him. He had to walk it home from the bicycle shop because he didn't know how to ride it. He didn't want to scratch it until his father had seen it. Wayne recalls that first ride as he pours the egg mixture into the skillet. His father stood on the curb watching as he hoisted himself onto the bike for the first time. But the seat was too high. His feet didn't reach the pedals properly and he could not gain control of the forward motion. The bike wobbled badly and his crotch thumped down on the crossbar, bringing tears to his eyes. He fell sideways, bringing the bike down on top of himself. By the time he got up and started again his father had gone inside. But he had continued and taught himself how to ride as well as anyone by day's end. And without the help of anyone.

"Hey, Dad, did ya see me?" George asks as he explodes into the room. "I was doing wheelies. Did ya see?"

"I saw. You looked great. You ready for food?"

"I'm starved."

As Wayne serves up the food, George watches his father

and wonders how to tell him how he feels inside. But the feelings are mixed up. A mixture of happy ripples and tugging fear that makes his stomach tighten up. Maybe saying anything would spoil everything.

They eat in silence for a few minutes.

"This is good, Dad," George says.

"That pan makes them just about perfect."

"Dad, can we save the cake for later? I'm full."

"Sure, I'll get some plastic wrap so it stays fresh."

Wayne gets up and covers the cake. He is aware of his son smiling as he watches.

"What's funny?" he asks.

"You. My dad."

"How come?"

"Sometimes . . . I don't know. Sometimes I forget that you're my dad."

Wayne sits down across from the boy.

"Because I don't pay enough attention?"

"No," George says. "You pay attention but you get things on your mind. I can tell. I sometimes try to figure out what you're thinking."

"Probably just daydreaming. Speaking of which, you better get going or you're going to be late for school."

"What will you do today?" George asks.

Wayne smiles at his son's curiosity. He had a similar curiosity when he was a child. He always wondered what his father did when he went out the door. Oh, he knew there was a job to go to, money to be earned. He knew what his father did, but it was the doing of it that fascinated him. Did his father like what he did? Who did he talk to when he was away? Did he whistle while he worked? Sing songs? Wayne had never asked his father about these things. They belonged to the man's privacy.

"What?" George asks again.

"Since I've been on sabbatical I don't plan much. But I'll have to teach some summer courses, so I should do some reading. Get some assignments ready."

"What're you really going to do?" George asks with a smile. A smile that contains just the right amount of charm and warmth without being phoney. A smile that startles Wayne because he cannot remember seeing it before and yet it seems familiar. He smiles back.

"Probably go play some racquetball. Take a walk. It's a nice day."

"Can I come with you?" George asks.

A strange panic races through Wayne and settles in his belly.

"You've got school," he says.

"It's my birthday," George says. "Make it like a present."

He stares at his father and will not let the man look away from his eyes. He fears saying more. He does not want to beg. His eyes must make his father understand.

"You remember when you were a little kid and we used to sit outside and watch the stars at night? In the summer."

"Yes," George says.

"And we used to make wishes on the first falling star. You remember that?"

"Sure, I remember."

"Do you remember what you used to wish for?" Wayne asks.

"No," the boy says.

"Neither do I. But we wished for something, didn't we?"

"Can I come with you today?" George says.

His father seems distracted, as if he has forgotten the question. George follows his father's gaze through the window to some far-off place on the horizon. He sits very still, hardly breathing, waiting.

"Why not?" Wayne says. "But you'll have to help clean

75

up before we go out. And go where I go. No complaints."

"No complaints," George says.

An hour later they are at the racquetball club. Wayne has booked a court and as he pays the woman behind the counter he is painfully aware of her questioning grin.

"Finally found somebody you can beat, eh?" she says.

"My son," Wayne says.

"Hey, I didn't know you had a kid," she says.

"It's his birthday."

"I'm eight," George says.

"Hey, great! Happy birthday. My name's Brenda. You should get your old man to bring you more often. Actually, he's pretty good. He should be. He's here every day."

George puts his hand out and after a few seconds the surprised woman grips it with her own.

"My name's George," the boy says.

"You got some kid there, Wayne," Brenda says.

"I know," Wayne says. "I know."

In the locker-room they change into shorts and running-shoes. They share one locker for their clothes, which makes George feel extraordinarily happy for some reason. He watches his father put a white sweat-band around his forehead and then carefully remove his racquet from its leather case and tests the tautness of the strings by banging them against his hand.

Wayne is conscious of the boy watching him.

"Ready?" he asks.

"Where do we go?"

"Follow me. Hey, why don't we trade racquets? Those rented ones are okay but mine's a pro model. Gives you a little edge."

They make the exchange, both of them grinning.

On the court, Wayne shows George how to serve the ball. He expects that they will just bang the ball around. For a few minutes they do, but then the boy catches the rhythm of the game and begins to volley with passionate energy.

"Hey, don't kill yourself," Wayne says.

"I like it. Come on, Dad, serve."

They play for 30 minutes, Wayne holding back but still working up a sweat and marvelling at his son's stamina. After a shower, they sit together in the whirlpool for a long time.

"That was fun," George says, "but it sure made me tired."

"You could get real good at it. You move fast."

"It's sort of a grownup game."

"I guess so."

"I'm glad you let me play."

"Me too."

When they are dressed, Wayne decides to have lunch in the club restaurant. He often eats there and thinks it will be a nice treat for George. He is surprised at how relaxed he feels. He thought he would be anxious with the boy along.

They find an empty table and are reading the menu when suddenly Wayne feels a pair of cool hands clamped over his eyes.

"Guess who," a voice says.

Wayne can hear George giggling.

"Barbara," he says.

"Right! So how do I look? Just started back today."

"I heard you had a girl," Wayne says. "Congratulations."

"That's right. Seven-and-a-half-pounds' worth. We call her Sarah. She's at home in the loving arms of her grandma. But who's this guy?"

"My son, George. And this is Barbara, our waitress, if she gets the time to take our order."

"So this guy's your father. Is that a fact? He never even told me about you."

George is beaming. And Wayne remembers a scene similar to this from a long time ago. With his father. In a restaurant. The only time in his life that he can recall being in a situation like that with his father. It was a restaurant that his father obviously frequented. The waitress had a nickname for him. They called him Foxy. They joked with him and one of them put her arms around him. He had been about George's age, just a little boy, and he had watched it all in awe. This was not the silent man he knew at home. This was a different person. His father had ordered pork hocks for him, something he had never eaten before. And, for that brief hour, he had caught a glimpse of a father he never knew he had.

"Hey, Wayne," says a passing man, "play a game next week?"

"You set the day," Wayne answers.

"Next Thursday, at noon."

"I'll be here," Wayne says.

"You sure know a lot of people," George says.

Wayne smiles at him and wonders if the boy will remember this day. Perhaps not, but *he* will. Already it has been a good day.

"I like having lunch with you," Wayne says.

"How come?"

"Because you're good company. And after we get out of here, I'm going to take you someplace special."

"Where?"

"A secret."

"Okay," George says.

A few hours later they are walking around the zoo. George feels slightly disappointed. It's not that he doesn't like the zoo, but he feels as if he's alone, even though his father is walking beside him. And he is worried about how sad his father looks. Even when he smiles, his eyes are still sad. And he has become quiet, hardly saying anything.

"Dad," George says, "are you sad?"

They are standing in front of an enclosure that contains a shaggy polar bear who is walking back and forth in an agitated state.

"I was thinking of your mother," Wayne says. "We used to come here all the time. Before you were born. We didn't have much money and it was a nice place to come. After a while though, we knew all the animals and it was sort of boring. Until she started to give them names."

Something inside of George unfurls. It is like something that has been smashed, but it takes a second for it to begin to fall. Great pressure from within is released and the sobs make his chest heave. He flings himself at his father, who holds him tightly while the tears flow.

"I wish she had never died," the boy cries.

And Wayne holds him like that for a long time. And then when the boy is breathing easily again he loosens his grip a little and even takes a step back so there is a gap between them. He gives the boy some Kleenex and turns to look at the bear while George blows his nose.

"She gave them all names," Wayne says.

"Names?" George says.

"Yeah."

"Like what?"

"This polar bear. She called him Posse."

"Posse the polar bear. That's a crazy name."

"She called him that because he's always looking behind. Looking over his shoulder. Like he was being chased by a posse."

The boy gives a faltering laugh.

"And then there was Oink, the owl," Wayne says.

"Oink the owl!"

"She said he looked like a pig with feathers."

The boy lets out a full laugh.

"Those sure are crazy names," he says.

"Your mum was a wonderfully crazy person."

"Could we make up some names?" George asks.

And from somewhere Wayne experiences a sense of relief.

"Sure we can," he says. "I don't remember all the names your mum made up."

George is dancing with excitement.

"Let's go to where they keep the orangutan. I want to name him first. I want his name to be Adam."

"How come?"

"Because he jumps up and down like an adam's apple in your throat."

"Hey, that's good."

The time passes quickly. It is evening and they are at home. Supper has been eaten, along with several helpings of the birthday cake for both of them. The new bike has been ridden and sustained its first scratch in a collision with a hydro pole. George is in his pyjamas, ready for bed. He feels very tired. Dreamy. He hugs his father briefly.

"Sweet dreams," Wayne says.

"I'll need a note for my teacher tomorrow," George says.

"I'll write one."

The boy begins to walk along the hall and then he turns back.

"That was the best birthday I remember," he says.

"Maybe we'll do it again next year," Wayne says.

"Okay," George says, and then he is gone up the stairs.

Wayne sits in the kitchen looking out of the window, watching the last light of day fade. And then it is dark. And suddenly an impulse seizes him and he gets up and hurries to the wall-phone. He dials the number and waits. After four rings it is answered. George's voice is sleepy.

"Hello," the boy says.

"It's me," Wayne says. "I love you, George."

"I know," George says. "I know." And then he hangs up and Wayne stands there listening to the dial-tone. Smiling.

## Pussy Willow

Wayne Maitland hovers on the brink of being in love. It is six in the morning and he has just witnessed the rising of the sun, feeling as he watched a lifting of the burden within himself. He attributes this to Bernice. Bernice, who each morning at just about this time plunges into the swimming-pool where she works and swims 200 lengths. She swims until the public pool opens at nine, when she assumes the role of lifeguard. The purpose of her early-morning work-out in the water is to ready herself for what she refers to as the paddle across the big pond. Lake Ontario. In August, just six weeks away, Bernice plans to swim across 30 miles of water, leaving from the American side and arriving at the Toronto beach just outside the grounds of the Canadian National Exhibition. She is aiming to touch shore inside Ontario Place, where tens of thousands could be on hand to greet her. Plus the television crews. She admits to hoping that a successful swim will earn her some money. It has for the few other people who have overcome the cold water, the throbbing cramps and fatigue so deep that it causes nausea and you have to be careful not to choke on your own vomit. So if money is forthcoming, Bernice feels it will be well deserved, but this is not the main reason for the swim. In the dozen times that Wayne has asked her why she is doing it, Bernice has always answered the same: "Because I imagined myself doing it."

Wayne leans against the railing of the second-floor balcony and smiles into the warmth of the new day's sun. He is amused to find himself at age 42 teetering at the edge of his emotions, almost ready to give himself over to them, and all because of an accidental meeting with a woman who is eighteen and earns her living as a lifeguard. A year ago, even a few months back, his life had been a trough of grief in which he wallowed. But now the grief and sorrow caused by his wife's death has receded. At moments like this, when he thinks of Wanda, of her absence from his life, it's with the same sense of awe and reverence as he has for the park across the street. The park stretches four city blocks and its very existence in the middle of downtown Toronto is astonishing to Wayne. As was Wanda's existence. The park is kept neat and tidy by grounds-keepers, but it is clearly not owned by anyone. As Wayne wanders the park late at night rediscovering old paths, spotting new landmarks, he sometimes thinks of Wanda and realizes that in life she was also unowned. Only in death did he try to possess her as if she were a piece of property that he could survey with certain instruments and then make a chart that identified every square inch of space she had filled. He had spent months rifling through his memories of Wanda looking for the deed, but then suddenly, and only very recently, he had come to see that he was like a robber looting his own house. His memories of Wanda already belonged to him and so he began to live easier and accept that he would not be able to make new memories with her. The same thing would happen when he finally moved from this house away from the park. He did not own the park but his memories of it, he did.

Wayne decides to ponder his hesitation about the state of being in love over a cup of coffee. The door from the balcony leads into the living-room, where Gloria, his daughter, and Gregory, her boyfriend, are asleep on the pull-out sofa. Gloria is sleeping on her back, the blankets forming a huge hump around her belly. The baby is already three days overdue but Gloria is snoring softly and giving no signs that a birth is about to take place. Gregory is a quiet sleeper and his thin body takes up little space on the bed. Wayne passes them quietly and slides along the hardwood floor of the hallway. The door to his office is closed. For the past few months Wayne's father has used it as his bedroom. Wayne puts his ear to the door and hears a low snuffling sound. It could be his father is having trouble breathing. Or the old man could be having a joke with himself. His father is not a weeper, even though cancer of the pancreas is devouring him rapidly. Wayne steps away from the door and makes his way to the kitchen, where he begins to prepare coffee. If his father needs him he will call out.

Wayne stands at the kitchen window looking out. There is a large bush in the yard that is in blossom. He gets a pair of scissors from a drawer and goes down the stairs to the side door, where he puts on his slippers before going out-side. The air is damp and the grass is wet with dew. He snips at the branches of the bush carefully so as not to spoil its shape. He has no idea what the bush is called, but the flow-ers are cream coloured, each with four petals that surround a centre dripping with yellow pollen. Wayne does not un-derstand his liking for flowers. It is not a liking based on knowledge. He is sometimes envious of those who can reel off the names of hundreds of plants, including the Latin title, but his desire to know has never been strong enough for him to make the time to study the subject. The colours are what seem to attract him. He takes the armload he has cut and heads back into the house.

The coffee is ready, its strong odour pervading the air. Wayne leans over the blossoms he is arranging in a vase and smells their fragrance. It is a sharply sweet smell that makes Wayne believe that the bush must produce some sort of fruit, but he cannot recall what it is. Perhaps the not knowing something so simple and obvious is partly what's wrong with him. He feels sometimes that he is drifting away, that he is becoming more and more an onlooker of life. And yet if this is true how is it that a bush that has grown outside his window for several years is a mystery to him? If he is becoming an observer wouldn't that be just the kind of thing he would notice more? It feels too early in the morning for such questions and his mood is shifting from a light-hearted, optimistic place within himself to a darker place.

He must get his mind back to Bernice. He pours a cup of coffee and in that moment he senses himself being watched. And he knows the observer is himself. He laughs nervously, pours a second cup of coffee and heads for his father's room in order to distract himself.

He pauses at the door and listens. He hears the raspy

breath but this is not unusual. In his 67 years of life Thomas Maitland has spent 50 of them smoking cigarettes. They have begun to take their toll. Wayne pushes the door open with his head. He is surprised to see his father half-sitting up, eyes open, one hand across his chest, his face squeezed as in pain and looking very old and somehow very young at the same time.

"I was just gonna call you," his father says.

"I brought you coffee," Wayne says and puts it down on the desk that serves as a bedside table.

"I wet myself," the old man says.

"Damn, you should have let them put that catheter in last week when we were at the hospital."

"I'm not about to walk around with a bag strapped to my leg. Sloshing with every step."

"Come on," Wayne says, tugging at the blankets covering the old man. "We'll clean you up."

"Drink your coffee before it gets cold," his father commands, hanging on fiercely to the cover. But Wayne tears it from him. And then he sees the blood. Pools of it, still wet and sticky.

"You're haemorrhaging. I'll call an ambulance."

"It makes me think of communion," the old man says, dreamily. "You know the way the priest mixes the water with the wine. My blood getting all mixed up with the rest of my juices. I'm not dying, sonny. I'm fermenting!"

He tries to laugh and begins to choke.

"Stop it!" Wayne shouts. "We've got to get you to the hospital. Something's ruptured inside of you. You'll bleed to death if we don't do something."

"I will anyway," Thomas Maitland says. "I can feel it happening."

Wayne recognizes the tone of finality in his father's voice. He feels frightened and angry. He does not want to witness the passing of another life and especially the life of this man, his father, a stranger.

"Don't send me away," his father says.

"Is there pain?" Wayne asks.

"It's more like a pressure, pushing on me."

"Can you roll over?"

"I think so."

Wayne puts his arms out and the old man pushes himself to the edge of the bed, loses his balance and falls. Wayne catches him and gently lowers him to the floor. The brown stains on his father's pyjamas blend with the dark carpet and give the impression that the man is disappearing in stages. Wayne moves rapidly to the bed and strips off the stained sheets.

"You've lost weight," he says, his heart pounding from the terror he feels.

"Setting an example for you. You could stand to lose some."

"I'll be right back," Wayne says. "You be okay?"

"I won't move."

Wayne goes to the bathroom and puts the soiled things in the laundry hamper. Probably throw them away later, he thinks. Later. When will that be? He grabs some clean sheets and a plastic mattress-cover from the linen-closet. He rushes back to his father.

"You okay?" Wayne asks.

"I'd like the bed better."

Frantically Wayne turns the mattress over. The other side is not as wet. He puts the plastic cover on and then the sheets. He puts his hand on it to check that the sheets are dry. They are. He then gets a clean pair of pyjamas from the small dresser and goes back to the bathroom for a damp face-cloth. Then he undresses his father and wipes the bloodstains from the old man's legs and thighs. When

87

that is done he puts the clean clothes on over the limp limbs and lifts his father back onto the bed.

"You're strong," his father says.

Wayne would like to tell him that he learned his technique nursing Wanda. But he feels cautious. His father saying he was strong could be a trick or a joke. Wayne didn't trust him.

"Do you need to go to the bathroom?" he asks. "I could carry you."

"I'm fine for now. Your coffee's cold. Get some hot."

"You want some?" Wayne asks.

"No. Just to watch you have yours."

Wayne takes the two cups to the kitchen and dumps them in the sink. He pours himself a fresh cup, goes back to the study and pulls a chair over to the bedside, where he sits facing his father.

"Light a cigarette," his father says.

"You want one?"

"I'd love one but it'd kill me." He begins to laugh again but then the bubbling cough erupts, shaking his body.

"Be still," Wayne says, and he lights a cigarette and takes a sip of coffee. He is unsure of what to do now. If he calls the hospital they will tell him to bring his father in. That's what happened with Wanda. They kept her alive for another week with a machine pushing air into her lungs and a tube down her throat. He waits for the coughing to stop.

"I'm afraid for George," he says when his father is finally quiet. "He's only eight. He watched what happened to his mother. It scared him."

"She died in the hospital. With all the machines. Scare anybody. Even me."

Wayne sits silently, something close to rage churning through his brain as he desperately tries to find a way out of the situation.

88

"When you were born, they didn't let fathers into the delivery room like now," Thomas Maitland says. "You know, like Gloria and Gregory are gonna do."

"I'm not sure they'll let Gregory in either. They're not married."

"I was there though. In the hospital. Even gave out cigars."

A slight shiver of shock passes through Wayne. His hand is shaking and he puts the cup down so his father will not see.

"I didn't know that," Wayne says.

"I got special leave to be there. Ten days later I was overseas. England. I sure loved that place. Even with the raids. And then Italy . . . "

His voice trails off but his eyes are bright as if he is seeing it all again. He smiles into the secret world of his past.

"You never came back!" Wayne says. "And then two months ago you show up. You get a doctor to call me from a hospital. The prodigal father returns. Kill the fatted cow, except maybe it should be a soft-boiled egg because the old man is old and doesn't chew too good with his false teeth."

Wayne stops, feeling as if he might burst into yelling. Or weeping. He gets up and goes to the kitchen for more coffee. When he returns it is with the belief that he has control of himself again. He sits down and lights another cigarette.

"You were almost six when I saw you next," Thomas Maitland says. "I was working as a cook on a freighter. On the Great Lakes. We carried grain from Port Arthur. I came to visit you on a layover."

"I don't remember," Wayne says, and he doesn't. There is a sadness within him that such a memory is lost.

"Your mother wasn't happy to see me. She was making a new life. I brought you a rubber ball. She tossed it into a bush. She had a temper, that woman."

89

"You never tried to contact me again," Wayne says.

"I kept track. From a distance."

"A long distance."

"I wasn't too good at loving in close."

Wayne feels a cloud of laughter rise from his stomach like steam. It is full of anger, hurt and sadness too. But it releases some of the tension in his taut muscles. He laughs loudly and the old man grins back at him.

"I guess that says it all," Wayne manages to gasp.

"Help me into the bathroom," his father asks.

Wayne picks up the frail man and carries him. He realizes that he has been oblivious to how thin his father has become. In the bathroom, he turns away and tries to close his ears to the sound of his father urinating. But when he flushes the toilet he sees that the water is a reddish colour.

"Does it hurt?" he asks as he carries his father back to the bed.

"A bit," the old man says.

"I'll get you one of the pain-killers."

"Not just yet. They make me sleep."

Suddenly there is the sound of running feet in the hall. Wayne is at the door of the study as Gregory flashes by, still only wearing his undershorts.

"Her water's broke!" he yells to Wayne. "All over the damn bed. Almost drowned me. I gotta call the hospital."

He disappears into the kitchen and Wayne can hear him dialing. He goes back to his chair and sits down beside his father. He has no idea what to do. Everything seems out of his control. And then George, fully dressed in his summer uniform of shorts, T-shirt and running-shoes, bursts into the room. The boy races over to his grandfather and leaps up on the bed beside him.

"I heard yelling," George says. "What's going on?"

"Your grandfather's sick," Wayne says.

"Gloria's going to have her baby," Thomas Maitland says.

"I'm gonna be an uncle today!" the boy shouts. "Can we all go and watch?"

And then Gloria herself, wearing maternity slacks and a tent-like top, enters the room carrying an overnight case.

"So this is where everybody's hiding."

She pushes a chair closer to the bed and sits down.

"The contractions are coming every nine, ten minutes. I think this is it."

"So at last I'll be an uncle," George says, grinning with satisfaction.

"Are you scared?" Thomas Maitland asks.

"Out of my wits," Gloria says, "but it feels like there's this motor inside me that keeps me running."

Gregory appears in the doorway.

"Doctor says we should get there. I'll get dressed."

"I can't drive you," Wayne says.

"But Gregory can't. He never learned. What's wrong?"

"My father's ..." What can he say? My father's dying and I want to be with him, except I don't.

"I'm feeling rough," Thomas Maitland says.

"Ya look kinda pooped," Gloria says. "I was hoping we could all be there for the big event."

"I did my stint in the waiting-room," the old man says. He grins at Wayne, who turns away from his father's look.

"Sure. Well, that's okay. Will you be all right on your own?" Gloria asks.

"Call a cab," Wayne says.

"Daddy, what's wrong? We had this all planned." Gloria looks like she is ready to cry. Wayne feels like screaming.

"He's just nervous about being a grandfather for the first time," Thomas Maitland says.

Gregory enters the room, dressed now and obviously full

of nervous energy.

"Shall we get this show on the road, folks?" he says.

"Grandpa's not feeling good and Dad doesn't want to leave him," Gloria says.

"He'll go with you," the old man says and he looks fiercely over at Wayne. "I want to ask you all to do something for me. Later. I'm telling you now in case I forget. You see those," he says, pointing at a vase of pussy willows that are sitting on the desk. They all look. Most of the silky catkins have fallen from the branches, but in their place have grown long strings of pale green leaves. "Pussy willows. I picked them down by the Don River more than a month ago. I like how soft the buds are. Take one out, Wayne."

Wayne gets up and lifts one of the branches from the vase of water.

"See," the old man says. "I put them there and while I forgot about them they rooted. Like magic."

The branch Wayne is holding does have a large number of white roots curling out from the skin of the wood.

Gloria bends in the chair as if seized by a cramp.

"Another one?" Gregory asks, fear in his voice.

She nods.

"We gotta get going," Gregory says.

"Plant them for me," Thomas Maitland says. "When there's time, plant them. Now go."

George is the first up and out the door. Gloria, supported by Gregory, follows. Wayne rises from his chair and kneels beside his father. He puts his arms around the man and hugs him gently and then kisses him for the first time in his life. His father smiles and Wayne leaves the room.

On his way out to the car, where the others are waiting, Wayne suddenly thinks of Bernice. He will call her from the hospital. Perhaps she can get away from the pool and be with him when he becomes a grandfather.

92

## The Ceremony of the Child

I sometimes feel like I'm traveling backwards into the future. Today my first grandchild will be christened. I'm excited about the event, but confused too. I wish there was something that stood between me and the actual experience. Like a movie camera. If I could witness the ceremony by looking through the view-finder of a camera I would be a lot more comfortable. Whatever happened to the Colgate invisible shield? I mean, I want to be there and I want to be seen to be there, but I feel like I need protection. I might break down and make a fool of myself.

The child is to be christened Thomas Wayne Maitland. Thomas after my father, who died just a month ago. I think he would be pleased. But amused too. He took things less seriously than I do. I'm a bit embarrassed that my daughter, Gloria, chose to give my name to the child as well. I tried to talk her out of it and she laughed and said she was killing two birds with one stone. I wish I was close enough to her to ask what she meant by that.

The whole situation is a bit unorthodox. Gloria is not married. She and Gregory, her boyfriend, live with George and me. George is my eight-year-old son. After the baby was born it was George who suggested I let Gloria and Gregory have my bedroom since it was large enough to accommodate a crib too. George is a smart boy. Smarter than me sometimes, which can be irritating, but the idea was a good one so I moved into the study and sleep on the same single bed that my father died in. I keep meaning to get rid of it, but during the day I forget about it. It's only at night that I remember and then it's too late to do anything. A couple of times I've slept on the floor to avoid the bed. It's not that I believe in ghosts but I've had several bad dreams in that bed. Dreams about disappearing. I have a fear of vanishing, emotionally speaking, I mean. A drinking pal once nicknamed me the Shadow. It was meant as a joke but I am aware of my capacity to withdraw.

Under the circumstances I was surprised that Gloria was able to find a minister to officiate at the christening, but she did. He's the same man who did the service at my father's funeral. He was recommended to me by the funeral director. I appreciated the restraint he showed in not lavishing praise where it wasn't due. After all my father was a stranger to him. To us all. So the words he spoke were, I thought, respectful without the inference of intimacy. He gave a certain dignity to the occasion that I felt inadequate to do.

Perhaps he would be able to do the same today at the christening. I hope so, for Gloria's sake. This is an important day for her. And for Gregory too. You see, Gregory is not the father. I mean the biological father. But today he will declare his commitment to the child and take on the responsibility of being its father. I admire Gregory for this. In his position I doubt if I would do the same. But I recognize that he loves the child separately from Gloria. He is not doing this to impress her. It seems to me to be an act of faith.

The ceremony will take place in the back yard. The minister seems satisfied with this. I offered to pay the church rental, because I know Gloria and Gregory are always broke, but they said they preferred this arrangement. George has scrubbed the bird-bath and filled it with clean water, and apparently this is where "small Thomas," as he calls the infant, will be baptized. It seems a little bizarre to me. Even sacrilegious, but again the minister has approved of this arrangement.

During the ceremony the three men will present the child with gifts. George has fashioned a marvelous bowl from clay that his teacher helped him glaze a bright red. It is supposed to be a secret but everyone has seen it except the baby. Gregory has written a new song that he will sing. No-one has heard the words, but he's been working on the tune for weeks and it sounds lovely. I'm afraid my gift is very traditional: an engraved silver cup and a tiny spoon for when Thomas begins to eat solid food from George's bowl. I wanted to be more imaginative, but I also felt compelled to acknowledge my real role in this little pageant. After all, I am the grandfather, a figure of stability. I have little experience in this role, so the silver cup and spoon are a kind of disguise.

The christening is to be a private affair. Gloria told me there was no-one else she wanted to attend. I was apprehensive that she would want her mother, my first wife, to come, but she said no. I'm not even sure that her mother knows that the child has been born. Gloria and her mother are not close. Gregory has not spoken to his parents in years. He assures me that they don't dislike him or he them, but no-one has shown a desire over the years to stay in touch. I find both their attitudes frightening. Gloria was raised by her mother until she was sixteen. Is she saying those years didn't count? Gregory left home when he was nineteen and it's as if his childhood was just something he grew out of, like a suit of clothes, and then discarded. But maybe they are the healthy ones. I dwell too much on the past.

I mentioned the possibility of inviting some of their own friends. I offered to have someone come in and serve up some sandwiches. After all, it's a special occasion and should be celebrated in a way that we'll all remember. They both thought my idea was pretty funny and told me if I wanted to splurge they would have their friends over for a party after the ceremony and I could spring for pizza and beer. I agreed but I'm still curious why they didn't ask their friends to be at the christening. I suspect that they're concerned about not embarrassing anyone. Maybe even themselves.

It is a gorgeous July day. The sun has just begun to cast its light into the yard. By three this afternoon, when the event begins, there will be no shadows dancing across the lawn as there are now. The sun will be in our faces, making us squint a little, and it will be hot so if there is the odd tear it will dry quickly. I am glad for the promise of good light and as I sit here in the kitchen, drinking coffee, smoking cigarettes and watching through the window, I am glad my daughter has asked me to be part of this day. I realize she has never asked me to join her in anything this important before.

They have taken the child for a walk in his carriage. It is

the carriage that I used to push George in when he was a baby. He's gone with them and I can imagine the three of them gently competing to see who steers as they push the old English pram through the park; other strollers insisting they stop so they can exclaim over the beautiful baby, and then the three of them continuing on again. And each of them smiling. Proud of something they could not explain.

I am waiting for them to return. The beer is chilling in the refrigerator. When the minister arrives I will phone for the pizza. It will take the restaurant about an hour to deliver it and by then the ceremony will be over. The party will begin. Most of the music will be played by Gregory, although some of his friends are musicians too. The songs will be old. And they will be sad. I am surprised at Gregory's obsession with sad music. He is not a sad person. In fact I would describe him as an optimist. He claims that he sings sad songs because people are more comfortable allowing themselves to feel pain. He believes people weep more easily than they laugh. I have argued with him about this, pointing out how easily I laugh but how difficult it is to cry. He smiled when I said that and put his arm around me for a moment; that kind of thing does not embarrass him. My laughter, he said, was a way of avoiding pain and all feeling. He may have a point, I suppose. I like it best when what I feel is a kind of numbness. Neither good nor bad.

The phone is ringing. I love the telephone. It allows me to connect with other people without any risk of consequences. If things get awkward on a telephone I can always hang up and blame faulty relay equipment for the break. Relating to people on the telephone gives me a tremendous sense of control. The only feature of the telephone I don't like is not knowing who is on the other end of its summoning ring. I wonder who could be calling me on this bright July afternoon. Perhaps it is Bernice.

A booming voice shouts at me as I pick up the receiver.

"Is Wanda there?" a man asks.

I am sure I recognize the voice.

"Arnold?" I say. "Is that you?"

"Yes," he answers. "Is that you, Wayne?"

"Yes."

"Can I speak to Wanda?" he says.

His request startles me into silence. It has been so long since anyone has called asking for Wanda. I feel a pinch of anger toward Arnold. He and Wanda grew up in the same neighbourhood and attended university together. They were good friends, but Arnold had the habit of wandering off in pursuit of his own dreams without telling anyone where he was going. He wouldn't write or phone and Wanda and his other friends would spend hours speculating about his whereabouts and even wondering if he was still alive. Inevitably he would reappear after a year or two and horrify everyone with stories about how he had contracted malaria in the tropics and been forced to treat himself with a special tea brewed from the bark of a tree because he couldn't afford to buy quinine. Arnold always assumed Wanda and his other friends would be in exactly the same place when he returned. I'm not sure if I resented him because he took Wanda and everyone else for granted or because his assumption about them was generally accurate. They were stable people and their lives did not take the dramatic lurches this way and that that his life seemed to. The last time Wanda and I had seen him he had just reurned from two years in India. Wanda was very ill, but he didn't seem to notice. He spent several hours with us telling entertaining stories about how he almost starved to death in Calcutta. That was more than a year and half ago. We hadn't heard from him since and there was nowhere he could be reached.

"Hey, Wayne," he says. "Get Wanda to the phone."

Obviously he had just returned from further travels and had not spoken to any other friends.

"Wanda is dead, Arnold."

"She couldn't be . . . " he begins to say but I interrupt.

"She had cancer the last time you saw her. She died a few months later."

"Where is she?" he asks.

"She was cremated."

"So there's nothing left," he says.

"Just George and me."

"She was so young. Just my age. I can't believe it. She never let on."

A curtain of silence is drawn between us. I feel I dare not comment on his remarks. I am angry with his carelessness and would wound him deeply for the pain his absence caused Wanda. But it would be pointless. Her death is history now. And probably what is bothering Arnold right now is that his existence had no influence on Wanda's fate. It's too late for him to do or even say anything.

"I feel awful," he says finally. "Just awful. I need time to think about it. I'll call again when I can talk about it."

He hangs up and I know I will never hear from him again. He will take his grief elsewhere and I'm grateful for that. I have had enough of grief, which for me was a process of discovering that part of my past was frozen. When Wanda died I remembered her with regret. It was a long time before I realized that the regret was not for the memories that she and I had shared but for the memories we could never make because she was gone. I guess grief in a way is the final letting go of certain possibilities. Like our youth. It is given to us and then it passes, never to be reclaimed.

In her last months of life, Wanda became very quiet and withdrawn. She took out a subscription to a religious magazine that was delivered weekly. She spent most of her time in bed because the disease had spread to her lungs by then and even walking to the bathroom was painful. She would sit up in bed and look out of the window into the yard. The religious magazine would always be open in her lap and occasionally I walked in and found her reading it. This surprised me since she had never expressed any strong religious beliefs. She did not belong to a church and although she attended services at Christmas and Easter she would always come home exclaiming about the beauty of the pageantry, the rousing music, the back-breaking pews. There was no mention of the spiritual content of the services, so I concluded she wasn't interested in that part. Bu then this religious material began to appear and I didn't know what to think.

Wanda and I were not talking much in those days. I knew she was dying. I suppose she did too. We were afraid. Even George, our son, was very quiet and spent a great deal of time playing outdoors and plotting ways to get invited to stay overnight at friends' places. I had a leave of absence from work so I could be there if Wanda needed me. We had very few visitors. It was a lonely time.

Week after week the small journals arrived. Wanda read them and then they were stored, secretly I thought, in a drawer of the bedside table. I felt the time disappearing. I had things I wanted to say but I had no idea if they were the right things. Finally I asked about the magazines she was getting.

"They have daily prayers in them," she said.

"But you . . . " I stumbled.

"What? I don't pray?"

"We've never talked about anything like that, Wanda."

She began to cry and I moved onto the bed and held her. After she stopped we both sat there staring out the window at the dogs rummaging in the back-lane garbage pails.

"I never learned to pray," she said. "Before I die I want to make my own prayers. The books help."

"Let me be part of it," I said.

"Do you pray?" she asked.

"I send out messages."

She laughed for a brief second.

"Who gets them?"

"I don't know. I don't think about it."

"Then why do you do it?" she asked.

"Because sometimes I need to put someone else on the hook for what's happening."

"God?"

"I guess so."

"What do you pray for, Wayne?"

"Relief," I said.

"I pray for life after death," she said.

"Heaven?"

"No, that doesn't interest me. I mean for you and George."

"I don't understand," I said and I didn't.

"I mean I don't want my death to diminish your lives."

It was the first acknowledgement between us of how ill she was. I felt weak with gratitude.

"This will sound crazy," she said, "but I think God is the future. I feel like the future's guaranteed in a way that I never did before. If you and George believe in the future, Wayne, you'll live. And if you live I will be part of the future too. I have to be!"

She began to sob deeply and she struck the pillow savagely. Over and over.

"You'll take me with you wherever you go," she said. "I'm part of you both. You'll never forget me."

Later that night Wanda woke me when the pain became too brutal for her to sleep. It was the first time she had done that. I stood with her in the warm shower and rubbed her back and held her as she wailed out her anguish. I tried to comfort her and I knew in that instant that she was right; I would never forget her.

The phone is ringing again. Probably it's Arnold calling back for more details. I've noticed that the close scrutiny of unpleasant news can sometimes lessen its emotional impact. Sometimes. Perhaps Arnold wants my help in pursuing this escape route. If it's him I'll just unplug the phone until after the christening.

"Hello," I say. I hear loud music in the background and then a male giggle. It is not Arnold.

"Wayne, I've put together the perfect suicide kit!"

This announcement is followed by loud laughter. I recognize the voice. It is Bill, an old friend who is obviously quite drunk and probably depressed. He laughs loudest when he's most depressed.

"Bill," I say, "how are you?"

"Listen, Wayne, I'm serious. I've got this kit. Sittin' right here. It's perfect."

"What's wrong?"

"Nothing. I just wanted to tell you."

Bill is George's godfather. If something were to happen to me, Bill would be responsible for taking my place. Wanda and I fought about this. She liked Bill but did not approve of him. For the role of godmother Wanda chose a woman who is generous with her love and absolutely dependable. Bill is neither. At age 35, he has spent fifteen of those years serving time in prison. Petty stuff that usually happens when he's drunk. Like the time he was urinating on the roof of a building and slipped and fell a floor, smashing through the skylight of the next building, breaking his leg and then being charged with break and enter because the office he landed in was that of a wholesale jewellery company. Or the time he and another fellow were enjoying a summer evening on the beach with two women and Bill decided a barbecue was in order, but it was three in the morning with all the stores closed and they had nothing to cook. Bill said he knew of a butcher's shop and they could kick in the back door and have their choice of the best steaks in the house. He was drunk, of course, and they broke into the wrong place. It turned out to be a fur store. They grabbed a couple of coats anyway and were arrested an hour later when the police discovered them on the beach using the coats as blankets. Bill got three years for that one. No-one was laughing. Except me, I guess, and probably my laughter was for all the wrong reasons. I wish I had the nerve to be as crazy as Bill. Wanda was right, a godfather should be someone sane and sensible. But I chose Bill. Maybe out of guilt. It's strange, Gloria and Gregory have not chosen godparents for Thomas Wayne Maitland. The reason they give is that their friends are too young to be trusted with such a big task. I don't buy that. I think the real problem is that they're not married and therefore have no clear way of delegating their responsibility. Gregory is talking about legally adopting the child. In the meantime, Gloria spoke to me yesterday and said that if anything were to happen to her, she wanted me to look after "small Thomas." Me and George, that is. The idea terrified me.

"You still there?" Bill asks.

"Yes, I was waiting for you to tell me."

"She left me, Wayne."

"Judy?" Judy is his wife of three months. A smart, determined young woman who thought she could reform Bill. There have been many others but Judy is different in that she is the kind of person who knows when to quit.

"I've got a bottle of vodka here. A 40-ouncer."

"It sounds like you've already had a few shots from it."

"Wayne, I'm telling you, I'm gonna go over to High

Park, find a tree, sit under it and I'm gonna suck back these 25 seconals I've got. Wash 'em down with the vodka. And then I'm gonna put this Walkman on, you know the kind with the earphones, find some nice music. And the last thing, the best . . . "

He lets it hang there for a moment. He sounds so pleased with his plan that I find it hard to take it seriously. But with Bill it's difficult to know. I'm not sure he believes in his own life. It's like he has to kill himself to confirm he's alive. I think his prison stints are like little deaths.

"The best thing," Bill continues, "is then I'm gonna handcuff myself to the tree. I'll leave one hand free so I can toss away the key . . . . "

"That'll be your drinking arm," I remark.

"That's right! So I can finish off the vodka, listen to the music, pass out and die . . . . So whatya think? Perfect, eh?"

A line from an old song that Gregory sometimes sings pops into my head. "Everybody's talking at me, can't hear a word they're saying, only the echoes of my mind . . . . "

"Bill, my grandson is being christened today. Gloria's named him after me."

"Hey, geez, I didn't even know she had the kid. Hey, so you're a grandad."

He laughs loudly for a moment and then his voice breaks as if he might be crying. There is the sound of snuffling and nose-blowing and then his voice back on the line again sounding weary.

"God, we're all getting old," he says. "Don't you feel it?"

"Sometimes, but today I feel pretty good."

"Proud, I guess," he says. "You should be proud."

"I am," I say.

"I didn't mean to pull you down."

"You didn't, Bill. I want you to come over tomorrow. For breakfast."

"I'm on a bit of a binge," he says. "That's why Judy left."

"So bring the bottle," I tell him. "There's liable to be a few big heads here tomorrow. You'll be in good company."

"Tomorrow, eh?"

"Will you be okay?" I ask

"Till tomorrow? Sure, no problem. It's next week, next month, the whole calendar waiting that kills me. Tomorrow I can handle."

"Come then. There'll probably be cold pizza and warm beer."

"I'm sorry I laid this on you," he says.

"I'm glad you called me, Bill. Bring the handcuffs with you tomorrow. I'm thinking about going on a diet. I might want to borrow them."

He is laughing when he hangs up and the laughter sounds solid.

It is quiet again. I get up and pour another cup of coffee. Through the window I can see that the sun has moved across the yard. The bird-bath, an old cement creation, cracked and pitted, has a sudden dignity in the bright light. I sit down again to wait the last few moments.

I have some slight inkling of how Bill might feel. Next week Gloria, Gregory and "small Thomas" are moving into their own place. George and I will be back on our own. For the past few months this house has been filled with the sound of my father's voice, and then Gloria, Gregory and finally "small Thomas." I am frightened of the coming silence.

I worry about how Gloria, Gregory and the baby will make out. The three of them go to Allen Gardens every day. It's not too far for a walk. Gregory plays his guitar and sings his sad songs for the people that pass. He leaves his case open on the ground and people throw money in it. I keep telling him his approach is out of style. No-one responds to that singing troubadour stuff any more. He laughs and jingles the heavy bag of change he has received that day. Some days as much as $20, he tells me.

They take the child with them. The park has a beautiful tropical garden inside a huge greenhouse and Gloria spends hours wandering through it with my grandson. When the child sleeps she knits. She sits on a bench next to Gregory, creating brightly coloured shawls that people buy as quickly as she finishes them. I cannot convince them that there is no security in this way of living. Gloria gently reminds me of the sixties when, from what she has heard, I did similar things. I guess I did and I survived. They will too, I suppose, and I'm always here to help them if they need it. But will I survive without them?

The phone again. There are days when it can be a nuisance. I answer it.

"Wayne," a woman's voice bellows. Bernice. "The date's set. Three days from now. Will you come? You promised."

"I didn't promise," I say defensively.

"Well, in my mind you did. Listen, how often do you think you'll get the chance to be beside somebody swimming Lake Ontario?"

"The whole idea is crazy."

"That's why I want you there. Please, Wayne. I need you there. I'm scared."

"Your coach, the weatherman, everybody says it's go?"

"Everything is perfect. I should get across in twenty hours."

Bernice is only a year older than my daughter. She bubbles with enthusiasm for life. That's what first attracted me to her. We are friends but not lovers. That is my choice, not hers. She is fixated with swimming the lake and has trained for three years. I feel like she is trying to swim into my life. I keep her at bay. Her youth frightens me. It's like she has an endless number of tomorrows while mine are limited. More likely my fear is of her demand for closeness.

"Will it be a big boat going across with you?" I ask.

"Gigantic," she says. "The coach has lined up a yacht."

"George will want to come," I tell her.

"I want him too. I want both of you to come. I told my parents you'd be coming."

"Okay, we'll come."

"Hurrah!" she shouts. "I got my way about something. Can I come over? I want to tell you all the details."

"Not right now, Bernice. Call me back later."

"What's going on? You entertaining somebody?"

I hate jealousy. It's one of the clubs we use to hurt people when we feel hurt by them. I don't want to hurt Bernice.

"Small Thomas is being christened today," I say.

"And I wasn't invited," she pouts.

"I didn't do the inviting, Bernice."

"I don't think Gloria likes me," she says.

"She didn't ask her own mother."

"I'm sorry, Wayne. I'm acting spoiled. It's just I want to see you."

"Call back in two hours. There's supposed to be a party. If everything's under control I'll take you out to a movie."

"Are you mad?"

"No," I say. "I'm happy for you, Bernice. About the swim. I feel very special being asked."

"You are special," she says softly and then hangs up.

I hear them on the stairs. George is first and he runs at me and gives me a tackling embrace.

"We saw a perfect puppy in the park, Dad," he says. "He would've fit in our place perfect. When Gloria and them go, can we get a dog, Dad?"

"I'll think about it," I say.

"Okay, you don't have to think about it today. Tomorrow's

**107**

okay."

I laugh and he runs down the hallway.

"I'm gonna change," he calls back.

Gloria and Gregory appear at the top of the stairs and right behind them is the minister. For some reason he is carrying the child.

"Hello, Mr. Maitland," he says heartily. "A perfect day for a baptism."

"Perfect," I say, pouring him a cup of coffee and then exchanging the cup for the child he is holding.

"I want to wash up," Gregory says. "Have I got a minute?"

"Take your time," the minister says, as he heads for the stairs. "I think I'll just go out and check the sanctuary, as it were." The two men are gone and I'm left holding a slightly damp grandson, with my daughter examining me with a serious look.

"I never thought of you as the grandfather until right this second," she says.

"I'm growing into it. By the time he's twenty I might not be bad at it."

"This has been tough on you, hasn't it?" she says.

"What?"

"Everything," she says. "Your dad dying. Wanda before him. Us being here. And now being made a grandfather."

"It's life," I say, feeling kind of stupid but not sure what else I can say.

"You know what's crazy? I've lost track of why we're doing this today."

She looks ready to cry, her face twisted with puzzlement. And then suddenly she thrusts her head against my free shoulder and nestles in tight against my neck.

"Tell me, Daddy," she sobs.

I hesitate. Afraid.

"I guess it's an act of faith," I say.

"In what?" she asks.

"Tomorrow."

And the three of us, all slightly damp, huddle like that for a long moment.

## Swim For Your Life

Bernice has been in the water for seven hours. She is swimming between 60 and 70 strokes a minute. A few minutes ago she finished her hourly feeding of honey and orange juice and began to vomit. Everyone got panicky and shouted advice at her. Or questions. I'm a question person myself. I stood at the rail and called out, You okay? She rolled onto her back and floated for a moment, ignoring all of us. The spotlight from our boat shone on her face, but all I could see was goggles and her mouth opening and closing rapidly as if she were gasping. And then her arm was raised in an effort to shield her eyes from the bright light. The bright, surgical beam remained and she signaled violently, her arm thrashing at the piercing circle surrounding her in the dark water.

"Take the light off her," the coach shouted from the escort boat.

One of the crew swung the light away from Bernice and directed it out into the lake so it formed an illuminated pathway for her. She began to swim again and within seconds had re-established her regular pace.

Why did I shout? She couldn't hear me. I am safe on the yacht with my son George. The coach wouldn't let me in the motorized dinghy that putters alongside her. I would distract her, he said. So I'm stuck on the deck of an expensive boat that's owned by a car dealer, watching an eighteen-year-old woman, who claims to love me, attempt to swim Lake Ontario. And there's nothing I can do to help her. Except maybe to act my age, which is 42. I can witness her feat from a distance and speculate as to how she must feel. But I will never know.

I wish I was cruising overhead in the Piper Warrior. I could keep radio contact with the yacht and get reports of her progress. If I flew low enough she might be able to see me as a guiding light in the sky. Then I would be doing something useful. But Bernice wanted me on the water. I doubt if I could have found a pontoon plane on such short notice and besides I'd never landed one, but the idea of being able to splash down beside her from the sky appealed to me. I'd even thought of having a banner made up that I could haul through the air that said something like, Go, Bernice, Go. I did check that out with air-traffic control and discovered you have to have a special permit. Bernice didn't like the idea anyway.

I guess what I'd like is the chance to do something as

sensational as her swim. It's kind of childish of me. Definitely not mature and supportive. If I could swim well, I suppose I'd be in the water beside her. Competing. Swimming for my life. To beat her. Or something.

"She's fine now," Joan says. "Probably took in a little too much air with her feeding. That can make you sick. She's swimming well now."

Joan is Bernice's mother. She is sitting calmly in a lawn-chair, sipping at a bottle of beer. I like this woman tremendously even though I don't know her well. She seems to have a vast supply of relaxed loving that she lavishes on whoever is in close proximity to her. I'm used to the intense type that accepts or rejects with fiery passion. Joan has a presence that just kind of laps up against you in a friendly, comforting way, like warm bathwater. The first time I met her I figured she'd target a soft spot and then inflict a mortal wound. After all, she's only five years older than I am. Bernice is her baby. Instead, after I was introduced, she pushed forward and hugged me. Just like that. As if she trusted her daughter's judgment.

"Tell me again why they put all that grease on Bernice," George asks and he begins to giggle. Joan has been telling him this story all afternoon. Ever since we set out from Niagara-on-the-Lake.

"So she won't get wrinkles," Joan says. "Can you imagine the wrinkles you'd have if you were in the water for 24 hours. You'd *be* a wrinkle."

"I get wrinkles if I stay in the bath for half an hour," George says. He's just turned nine and is fascinated with his own body.

"Speaking of tubs," I say, "it's long past your bedtime."

"I wanna watch Bernice swim. You said I could."

"She'll still be swimming in the morning," I tell him.

"How far does she got to go now?" he asks.

112

Kids are terrific at diversions. But a certain pain from the past clutches at my consciousness and I need to be alone with it. A tide of sorrow distracts me from the immediate situation and I only need a moment to fight it off.

"You go to the cabin," I say. "Start to get ready and I'll be down in a minute."

"You didn't answer me."

"Hey, I've got an idea," Joan says. "It's my turn in time too. Why don't I pack you off to your bed and I'll even tell you the story of Gransel and Yetel."

"That's Hansel and Gretel," George says.

"Oh, not that story. This one's about a couple of children who run away and get lost in a video arcade. Not that soppy one about the witch in the candy house."

"So what happens?" George asks eagerly.

"Say good night to your dad."

"Don't drink too much, Dad," he says as he kisses me, "and don't forget to bring Sally to bed when you come."

I am barely aware of lips pressing against my skin, my eyes are drawn to Bernice's arms, rising and falling as she pulls herself through the water. I feel hypnotized by the movement and my hand reaches out for the glass of brandy and brushes up against Sally, who groans slightly in her sleep and automatically licks my hand. I take a swallow of the drink and hope it will burn the images from my mind. I wish I were a fourteen-year-old dog like Sally, my memory blurred, my sleep dreamless. But the motion of Bernice's arms beckons me. I stand and move to the rail, where I can see more clearly her twisting, turning body. And I remember.

I stood in the doorway and watched the nurse empty a syringe of valium into the intravenous tube that fed into Wanda's arm. It was the third shot in less than an hour and still my wife lifted herself and pushed against the restraints, her body writing for relief. I was terrified of it all. The respirator wheezed as it pumped air into her failing lungs through a mask over her face and a tube in her throat that had just been installed the day before. Slowly she relaxed and finally even her hands were still. The nurse moved quickly out of the way as the young doctor entered the room. He looked at me and I knew he wanted me in the room. I did not want to be part of this. I felt it was unfair for him to ask me to help him. I wanted to run and join the others in the waiting-room, but instead I took my place on the other side of the bed. For a moment I thought she was dead already, but then I took her hand and felt its warm shape curl around mine.

"Wanda," the doctor said. "Can you hear me? It's Dr. Franklin. I know the drugs have relaxed you, but I believe you can still nod. Will you nod if you can hear me?"

Wanda nodded.

"Good," he said. "Wanda, Wayne is with me. Your husband and I have talked and he thinks it's best that we tell you what's going on. It's not good news, Wanda. We thought you might have an infection, but it's the tumour. It's in both lungs. That's why we had to put the tube in to help you breathe."

He stopped and Wanda's eyes fluttered open. She stared fiercely at him and her anger was like a challenge. She knew the truth but could not utter her rage. Her eyes spoke the protest of a child who understands defeat but will not accept it. Or perhaps she did not look that way at all. It might have been the soft light reflecting in the moisture of her eyes that made them appear to glint. She might have been crying and the angry one was really me.

"Do you understand what I'm saying?" the doctor asked.

Again she nodded and then he too shook his head ever so slightly as if he was trying to find an equal footing with her.

"We need to make a decision," he said. "The machine is breathing for you. That's causing you part of the pain. We know the pain is bad, but if we turn off the respirator we don't know how you'll do on your own."

Wanda's hand moved within mine and shaped itself into a fist. She began to nod her head and this time I saw for sure she was weeping.

"Are you nodding yes for us to turn off the machine?" the doctor asked. "Do you understand what that means?"

Her head made an affirmative motion. And then the doctor turned to me.

"And you, Wayne, understand the implications and you concur?"

"Yes," I said.

Then, for the first time, the young doctor put his hand on Wanda. He placed it on her shoulder, just for a second, and his face was unmasked for that brief time and revealed a tenderness that bordered on tears.

"Good luck," he whispered.

He left the room quickly and for some reason I followed him. He stopped and pointed me back to the room. I looked and saw Wanda, her head turned toward me, the mask over her face, the tube in her throat taped to the side of her mouth and her arm waving, beckoning furiously to me to return. And I did. And I waited with her for several more hours, fearful to move, afraid that waving arm would follow.

A light drizzle is falling and the lake is choppy with small waves. The wind cuts through my light clothing and chills me. I'd like to go inside to a warm bunk, but that somehow seems disloyal to Bernice, who is still pounding her way through the water. Her coach and the young man who has come along to pace her are shouting encouragement but with the earplugs it's unlikely she can hear. She is in her own world. I watch her arms dipping, pulling her forward.

I remember my jacket on the chair, put it on and pour myself another large brandy. I suddenly hear Sally barking. She's at the far end of the boat with her head hanging over the edge. I walk to her and realize her agitation is caused by having no place to relieve herself. I point to the deck and finally have to bend down and tap at a spot before she gets the idea. Sheepishly she squats and I hurry back to my deck chair and drink. She joins me in a few moments with an appropriate look of guilt on her face. After all, up until a week ago, Sally had spent her fourteen years living with a psychologist.

I first met Sally's mistress several months ago when my doctor decided I was becoming jumpy and a bit fixated about Wanda's death. I guess he had a point. I had developed this peculiar habit of taking the aircraft up on long solo flights during which I drank large amounts of straight whisky and imagined turning off the engine and just drifting into a cloud. A couple of times I had shut down the power and almost cracked up. It couldn't have been too serious though because I told my doctor. If I had any real intentions I would have kept it a secret. Anyway, he referred me to Janet.

She worked out of her house, which surprised me a bit. At $50 an hour I figured she could afford an office. The first thing I noticed about her was the giant, dimpled smile she could flash in such variables of intensity I thought it was on a dimmer switch. But then I met Sally, who had bad breath and walked sideways as she approached you, so it took her a long time to get anywhere. Janet never smiled at the little blond dog, so I knew her affection for it was real. And before the first session was over I understood why she worked out of her home. Sally didn't like to be left alone.

The first few times with Janet I felt awkward. Something about that smile I didn't trust. It made me think of a cannibal. I rambled around in the things I said and she never stopped me. I didn't find it helpful. And then, on the third visit, just as I launched into yet another reliving of the funeral scene, she held up her hand to stop me.

"You have a vivid memory," she said. "You remember it all. In such detail. And yet, you don't feel it. You choke yourself with trying to remember more and more of the horror details. And I suspect what you don't recall, you imagine until that too becomes real. But you don't feel any of it, do you, Wayne?"

"No," I said.

"I want you to do something. Something that might hurt. I want you to tell me about you and Wanda when you were alive together. Before she was sick."

I didn't like the sound of that. I was used to death and dying. I never thought much of the earlier days. There didn't seem to be much point in dwelling on that time. Still, I didn't have an argument against it.

"I'll try," I said.

"Good. So tell me."

I felt very nervous all of a sudden and I was glad when Sally came over and licked my pant-leg. I felt encouraged and it made me think of something funny, which is often what I do when I feel nervous.

"There was this pig," I said.

"Yes," Janet prompted. She did not laugh but a low-beam smile flitted across her face.

"Some friends of ours were getting married. They wanted to do it at our place because we lived beside a river. They wanted a water wedding. So Wanda and I said sure. And then we got excited about it and I suggested that we bar-

117

becue a pig. We'd never done anything like that. So we rented this sort of industrial-size barbecue and I ordered a small pig from the butcher. Wanda came with me when I went to pick it up. I remember it was a beautiful July day and I had all the windows in the car open. The pig was about 70 pounds but it was bulkier than I thought it'd be. The butcher had it in a plastic bag and Wanda made me put it in the front seat. When we got driving she took my sun-hat and sun-glasses and put them on the pig. She had him propped up beside her, right next to the window so when we stopped for traffic lights people in the next car would look over and see this rather spiffy-looking pig with a strange woman next to him, grinning like a demented wolf. And waving at them. None of them waved back.

Anyway, we got up the next morning at five to light the barbecue and stuff the pig. There was this old guy who had a cabin just a little ways from our place and in the two years we lived there he hardly talked to us. He always thought of us as slobs. But that morning he came over and brought us apple strudel, still warm from the oven. And when we got the pig cooking, Wanda and I sat on the dock and we watched the sun burn the mist off the river. Drinking coffee and eating the strudel. On the other side of the river there was a family of herons fishing in the shallow water. And occasionally we'd see a bass jump. I remember it felt... restful.

The wedding wasn't until four in the afternoon, so we took turns having naps with the other guy basting the pig. By the time people started to arrive the smell of the roast-ing meat was hanging in the air and the skin was turning gold and getting crisp.

Our friends had found this minister who was perfectly legitimate but for some reason he'd agreed to marry them the way they wanted. I expected he'd arrive wearing a robe and love-beads but he had on a suit and his collar.

The minister took our little boat and rowed out to the middle of the river. The bride and groom paddled out in inner tubes. So did the best man and maid of honour. They were all wearing bathing-suits. Richard and Pam, the people getting married, wanted to do it that way because they believed that love had to flow like a river. That's what they said and who was going to argue? So the minister stood up in the boat and conducted the ceremony. The river isn't that wide and voices carry across water, so those of us on the shore could hear most of it. While that was going on, the rest of us were stripping to our bathing-suits so the second the minister pronounced them man and wife we all jumped in the river and swam out to congratulate them. There were about 50 of us and I noticed the old man from the cabin next to us watching. I guess we looked a little crazy to him.

Pam and Richard had arranged for some musician friends to come and after the pig was devoured and a little wine drunk there was this lovely guitar music. Soft acoustic, with someone singing a Valdy song. The stars were bright over our heads and we were dancing on the lawn, warm again in dry clothes with good food and drink in us. And Wanda was in my arms, her head resting on my shoulder, singing the words in my ear: Whirl, Swirl and Twirl, like drops of water. Dance through the fields with your sons and your daughters. Your sons and your daughters.... Grab your wife. Swim for your life.... As time goes on, time waits for no-one...."

I had to stop there because for some reason I was crying. God, I hate to cry. It feels so indulgent. Janet handed me a Kleenex and Sally tongued my ankles. Anxiously, I thought.

"You have marvelous recall," Janet said.

"I wish I could forget it all," I replied.

"Yes," she said, "but grief needs to know what has been lost."

We sat in silence for a while. Then she got up and went over to the small bar and poured herself a drink. She drank half of it with her back to me. I got up to leave. She turned and her smile faltered.

"We're finished for today," Janet said. "Stay awhile. Have a drink. Relax."

"Sure," I said.

I had several drinks. And I stayed a long time. I stayed long enough to hear Janet's story. The way she understood it. The way she remembered it. It was a sad story, I suppose. A story of several marriages that rusted out and then fell apart. And then a man appeared who inspired passion and trust. She lived with him for three years while he slowly drank himself to death. He had been dead just over a year and she was still trying to understand it. To accept the way it had ended. Like me with Wanda. She joked about being left alone again except for Sally, the dog, who was fourteen. It troubled her that the relationship with Sally was the only one that had lasted. I saw it as proof that dogs are more loyal than people.

It was a long evening and it was the beginning of what became a ritual. Janet would listen to me recount stories of the life that Wanda and I had made for ourselves. She insisted that I recall the happy, joyous times. Often I would finish with tears in my eyes. I hated the process and yet I was kind of addicted to the result, which was the feeling of pain. It was better than being numb. And then it was Janet's turn. The trouble was, her story was always the same. The details didn't change. Probably it was the booze that put her in a rut. I felt like a priest when late at night she would confess that the solution to her pain was to replace it with another. She wanted to marry again. As soon as possible.

Someone just had to ask her. Anyone. Almost. It didn't seem to matter that she might be repeating the same mistake. I thought that was kind of spooky.

The night Janet suggested that she and I might make a marriageable match, I thought it was a joke. She pointed out that I had the son and she had the dog. What a team we'd make. I laughed and she cried. I felt terrible and I stopped seeing her.

"Wayne, are you asleep?"

It's Joan, wrapped in a blanket against the cold. She walks to the rail and I see her take out a stop-watch. She is timing Bernice.

"How's she doing?" I ask.

"Slowing down," Joan says, and then she walks back to the chair and sits down. She produces a glass from the folds of her blanket and holds it out to me.

"I'll have a little brandy, please."

"Are you worried for her?" I ask as I pour the brandy.

"Yes, but only for what happens after," she says.

"Maybe she won't make it."

"Only if the weather doesn't hold or some crazy catastrophe happens. But that will only delay it. She'll try again. And again. Al will push her."

"The coach?"

"Sure. It's his dream to open a school for swimmers. Bernice is his ticket."

"Did you try to stop her?" I ask.

She laughs and startles Sally, who starts to bark.

"Shut up," I shout.

Sally stops and lies down again.

"That is the saddest-looking dog I've ever seen," Joan says. "You ever look at her eyes?"

"We just got her a week ago."

"She seems old."

"She's fourteen."

"Why didn't you get a pup? She'll die and break George's heart."

"I didn't intend to get a dog, period," I say, "but I had this therapist and a few weeks ago the wife of an old friend of hers died in England. So she flew over to give the guy support. Commiserate with him. You know. Anyway, she called me last week from London and said, Surprise. The guy she had gone to help through his rough time had proposed."

"So where does Sally fit in?"

"Well, when Janet called she told me she hadn't accepted the guy because she had this problem. She didn't mind giving up her practice and her mother could sell the house, but Sally, the dog, would have to go into quarantine for six months if she came to England. And that's where this guy wanted them to live. Also, Janet wasn't sure Sally would even survive the flight over. So, since George and I were looking after Sally anyway, I said we'd keep her. Sally would have a good home and Janet could get married. Simple. And Janet agreed and that's how we got Sally."

"Was this woman in love with you?" Joan asks.

It's my turn to laugh now.

"No," I say. "She just wanted to get married."

"Would you have known, do you think?" Joan says.

That's a tricky question and one that makes me feel uneasy.

"I'm sorry," Joan says, passing her glass to be refilled. "That was a silly question. You were asking if I tried to stop Bernice. I didn't but her father did."

"Is that why he didn't come?"

"He's like you in a lot of ways," she says. "Totally self-sufficient. He hasn't eaten a thing I've cooked in years. Of course he works those crazy shifts at the airport. I don't see him much. He even does his own laundry."

"Why didn't he want Bernice to do the swim?"

"He's afraid he'll lose her."

"Is that the same as the after you're worried about?"

"Yes. He thinks she'll become a celebrity and be sucked into some kind of life he can't be part of. I'm worried that she'll become a celebrity and it won't mean anything to her."

"But she's not doing this to become a media sweetheart."

"I know that," Joan says, "but it comes with the territory. Al wants the publicity and for a while, when the swim is finished, Bernice won't have a choice."

"Maybe she should go away."

"Will you take her?" Joan asks. And then she laughs as if she recognizes the threat in her question. She pats my arm to reassure me, I guess. "You don't have to answer that," she says, "but I wonder, how do you feel about Bernice?"

"Protective," I answer.

"Yes. You would. Her father and you would make good guards if she ever became a princess or a movie star. Nobody would ever get close to her with you guys around. I once told him he should open a takeout stand for unrequited love. We could call in our order and then drop in and pick it up. Save everybody a lot of time."

"You think I'm like that?" I ask.

"I think you got hurt when your wife died and now you're scared."

"What about your husband?"

"He got damaged a long time ago. He never knew how to deliver. He tries. I think it's different with you. You're close to George. Not as close as you could be. You hold him off too. But it's mostly women that seem to scare you so badly."

I try to smile away her observation. She passes me her

empty glass and I slop some brandy into it.

"What makes you hang in?" I ask.

"I have a good life," she says. "I learned a long time ago that I was the only woman that Jack wanted to be with. He has trouble being with anyone. And it was me that he chose to try the hardest with. I love him for that. And I have Bernice, who I think is like me. I mean, she'll survive no matter what. If you withold the love she wants from you, she'll find it elsewhere."

"She's so young," I say.

"You need to work again. Get back to teaching. Or write a movie. Even a book. Put your passion somewhere."

"Is that what this swim is to Bernice, a place to put her passion?"

"Partly," Joan says. "But it's also a way to conquer the loneliness she knows she'll face."

"Why should she be lonely? She's young, beautiful. In a couple of hours she'll be a star."

"I don't have the answer," she says, getting up. "But I see it every day on the wards, Wayne. Lonely, frightened people. That's why I love being a nurse. I put my hand on them and they smile. For maybe a second they forget to be scared. It helps make me braver too."

She walks over to the rail again and I get up and join her. Bernice has stopped to take a feeding. She sees us and waves. I see her mouth move but I cannot hear the words. She pushes away the pole with the feeding-bottle, makes an adjustment to her goggles and starts to swim again. The young swimmer in the escort boat dives in and swims beside her. Her pace quickens. They seem to be racing each other. The spotlight dances on the water in front of them. The small boat's engine putters softly and its rhythm in my ears makes me feel suddenly sleepy.

"She is a lovely girl," Joan says.

"I'm gonna go to bed," I say.

"Go ahead, Wayne. I want to stay up for a while."

Sally follows me and waits until I squeeze into the bunk with George, and then she jumps up and finds a space at the end of the bed. I think of Bernice in the cold water, smiling, her arms reaching out and pulling her forward into the gloomy darkness. I begin to fall into the shadows of sleep and I meet Wanda.

We were on the river. Each of us in an inner tube. A big ChrisCraft passed by on its way down to Lake Ontario. The people on board waved and smiled. Wanda and I rode the waves of its passing and laughed. We let the current carry us downstream. Wanda was wearing her straw hat with the red ribbon as protection against the hot sun. I had on my captain's hat. We didn't speak and when she drifted past the creek where we always turned I didn't shout. I thought perhaps she was day-dreaming and hadn't noticed. Any second she would turn back. I swung my tube around and began to paddle with my arms. I faced her and signaled for her to come back. She waved and I think she even grinned, but she kept floating farther and farther away. I saw with terror that there was a bend in the river. She reached it and disappeared. I paddled home, my arms chopping the water furiously, the anger like an engine, pulling me.

There's a lot of noise overhead. Shouting. I sit up quickly and see the bed is empty. I put on some clothes and run up on deck. There are boats everywhere, their horns hooting, bells ringing. But they're too close. They almost have Bernice's way blocked. Joan is at the rail screaming.

"Get back! Get out of her way!"

Al in the escort boat is using the feeding-pole to push boats aside. We are very close to the shore. I can see Ontario Place and the ferris-wheel at the CNE. Bernice is flounder-

ing in the water. Her goggles are up and she is being sick. I
can see why. The water is slick with diesel fuel and the fumes
hang everywhere in little clouds. The boats are crowding in
and people, oblivious of the shouted warnings, are leaning
over with their cameras to get a picture.

I go over to Joan, who is crying with frustration. George
is with her, standing on the rail, yelling.

"Get outa here, ya creeps!"

"They're going to ruin it for her," Joan sobs.

I put my arm around her. Try to offer some comfort.

And then something wonderful happens. A Harbour
Police launch arrives on the scene. It makes its way into the
cluster of boats and then stops. A man wearing a heavy
raincoat speaks through a megaphone.

"Clear the way," he says. "Immediately. Or we'll clear
you."

The boaters ignore him and he signals to three men on
the deck of his craft who are also wearing the heavy rain-
coats. They swivel the huge water-cannon mounted on the
deck and take aim at the nearest boat, which is only about
ten feet away. They fire the pressurized stream of water that
is used for putting out marine fires. The passengers scream
as the water hits them and knocks them down. There is the
sound of glass breaking. And then the offending boat's
motor revs up and they move quickly out of the way. Other
boats do the same. One persistent speedboat gets sprayed
and is almost capsized before its owner catches on that
these guys are serious. Within seconds there is a clear path
for Bernice. But Bernice is not swimming. She has drifted
close to the yacht and is looking up at her mother.

"You can make it, Berny," Joan says. "You're almost
there."

"I can't, Mum," Bernice says and her voice is feeble.

Other people are shouting encouragement. Al, the coach,

126

the young pacer, some of the crew and even George, but Bernice just bobs up and down in the water, unable or unwilling to move. Joan slips off her robe and hands it to me. She has on a bathing-suit and she steps over the rail and dives into the water. Bernice watches as her mother swims toward the shore. And then she grins, a weary, stubborn grin that contains no mirth but only determination. She adjusts her goggles and very slowly begins to pull herself through the water. A chorus of shouts fills the air. Bernice is closing in on Joan, who has never looked back since she dived. George takes my hand and squeezes it.

"She's going to make it, Dad," he says.

I feel a great pride at this moment. For Bernice. Her mother. The Harbour Police. All of us. I think it's simply the pride of being alive and feeling it.

We are less than a quarter of a mile from shore when this crazy notion takes hold of me. I grab the life-preserver from its hook and fasten it around my middle. Bernice and her mother will be touching shore in a minute or two. The cameras and newspeople will consume them. I want to know what it was like for them that last little way.

"George, I'm going to jump in. You wanna come?"

He looks at me suspiciously as if he expects a trick. And then he smiles and I notice how bright the sun is overhead. We shouldn't freeze.

"Can Sally come?" he asks.

"Of course," I say. "We'll all float in together."

I climb the rail and leap into the air. I hear George laughing behind me.

# Rural Ghosts

I have never been a believer in ghosts. Up until recently I would have had the impulse to laugh if anyone mentioned the possible existence of spirits. Beyond what you find in a whisky bottle. I've had plenty of encounters with that whimsical crew when my wayward mind, besotted with booze, has turned a corner of its own making and doubled back with old memories in tow, costumed in horror and determined to terrify me. The fears, I call them. Regurgitated past mistakes that dance through my imagination like a grotesque vaudeville act. A kind of psychic punishment for remembering too much. And too frequently. I suppose it's a kind of suicidal navel-gazing where the events that compose the landscape of my life are judged as if they were buildings being considered for demolition. It is an act of condemnation. But not to be taken seriously.

When I am sober I can dismiss these spiritual visitations as being purely chemical in their origin. An outside force trying to rattle me. In a day or two my stomach settles and my existence is no longer dependent on receiving hourly cups of chicken-noodle soup. Aspirin clears a path through the debris of my mind, where dynamite seems to have been used to destroy the myths of yesteryear. But soon I am wading into the dry crackers and my hand is capable of holding a cup of coffee without dumping half of the contents into my lap. As I recover through ritual eating, concentrated staring out of the windows and many naps, the memories propelled by guilt slowly recede and become a vague whir of emotions that a good exercise program can keep under control for months.

I do not recommend drinking spirits of any type as a way of getting in touch with the past. In fact, I believe the past should be avoided at all costs. It's a place that's filled with unfulfilled wishes. Yesterday's mistakes wait for you like a precision bugle corps, all lined up, instruments shining and ready to play their sickly selections, which will remind you of where you went wrong. The past contains your greatest disappointments. Going there is like visiting Disney World on a day when the Shriners have booked the whole place. You can see the magical world of your dreams and almost touch them, but you're locked out. You feel a rush of longing. Sadness. Or, if you're like me, anger. Rage even.

I work very hard at avoiding the past. When I was a child, an adult gave me some excellent advice: think about something else. Most of the time I do. But occasionally, for no particular reason, I find myself drawn back. It's as if I become lonely for all that pain and misery I left there. And I can't resist. I might do it with booze. A dozen drinks will do. Or I may just float off some rainy afternoon when I'm wtching a squirrel prowling its tree. My defences down. Caught off guard. And in less time than it takes to listen to a recorded Dial-a-Prayer message I've drifted into that discarded dreamtime zone. I scrounge about among the details of things that once delighted me trying to salvage perhaps a twinkle of hope for the present. Or the future.

Recently I came to believe in ghosts. One at least. Ghosts are witnesses of the past. They have no opportunity for dreams of the future. Their present existence depends on finding someone who will lock in with them to the past. I guess it gives them something to hang onto.

My wife Wanda died two summers ago of cancer. When the doctor first gave a diagnosis of cancer, he explained the disease was of a passive nature. It could not live on its own. It needed a host on whom it could depend totally for its existence. Cancer was like a lover who can never get enough of your vitality. The energy and exuberance that made Wanda so attractive in life were probably the very things that made her so susceptible to cancer. She was the perfect host. Open and giving. And the cancer took it all.

I think since the time of her death that Wanda's ghost has possessed me. Like a kind of cancer, gnawing at my energy, directing me away from the present into the past, where her existence had substance.

This is not a litany of blame. I loved the woman and it was my fear of life without her that allowed me to be possessed. Now I needed to find a way to take myself back. An act of reclaiming myself.

Yesterday I sold the airplane. I took it up for a circle of the city and when I returned I mentioned to one of the mechanics that I might sell it. He made me an offer. It was fair, so I accepted. Perhaps some day I will have another plane, but it will be one that I will fly with a destination in mind, not to escape.

Tonight I have my whole family with me, gathered around the kitchen table with the sun coming through the window to light their faces, which glow with golds and reds and browns. There is the pleasant smell of food and flower blossoms mingling lightly in the air. The voices of my family sound gently around the room. Chairs are pushed closely together. Only I remain outside the field of touch, but then small Thomas, my four-month-old grandson, almost topples from his little support-chair that sits on the table and I reach out to steady him and I too am connected with the others.

"Hey, you guys, I've got this idea," I say.

Gloria, my daughter, gives me an earnest but guarded look. I am still on trial with her, I think, but less so than before. I marvel again at the steadiness she has achieved in the last few months. She seems to me completely grown up and I regret it a bit. Gregory flashes a smile at me that is full of warmth and interest. Gregory has made a big difference in Gloria's life. Their living together has the smooth rhythm of a well co-ordinated dance. It is Gloria's doing that they are not married. She has learned caution from me. George, my son and living memory of his mother, reaches excitedly for my hand. I can even hear the thumping tail of our dog, Sally. She's probably anticipating a ration of human food.

"So what's up, Dad?" George asks.

"Summer's half over," I say. "I was thinking of us all taking a trip."

"That's great!" George says. "Can we go fishing?"

"Sure," I reply.

"Where to?" Gloria asks.

"I was thinking out West. Drive to the coast. Take our time. Camp. Stay at hotels when we feel like it."

"I couldn't afford it," Gregory says.

"I'll pay. It'll be my present for everybody."

"The thing is," Gregory says, "I've been getting a fair bit of studio work lately. Just fill in and I've been playing bass three nights a week at the club. I feel like I'm building a reputation. I wouldn't want to lose the momentum."

Gregory is a musician. A good one, and he plans to make it his career.

"I understand," I say. "But the rest of us could go. You wouldn't mind, Gregory, would you?"

"Hey, no. Full steam ahead."

"Excuse me if I put my foot on the brake, Dad," Gloria says. "What's this all about?"

She is staring at me, her eyes like front-end loaders ready to demolish any facade I present. I try to laugh lightly and look away but her gaze follows me like a laser beam.

"I thought we could have a holiday and at the same time visit some of the places Wanda and I went on the first trip we made twelve years ago. Sort of a . . . "

"It's morbid, Dad. What are you trying to do, take snapshots at the spots where she once stood? You can have them developed and have something to be depressed about all winter."

Everyone is quiet. There is a possible truth in what Gloria has said but of course I intend the trip to free me from the very morbidity she speaks of. But how to explain it?

"I'll go," George says quietly. "She was my mum, not Gloria's. I don't mind."

"Oh shit. Now I feel like crap. I just meant, like old Thomas died. We all loved him but somehow nobody's hung up thinking about him all the time. We're still living our lives. Except you, Dad. Over Wanda. You know what I mean?"

I laugh, genuinely thinking of ghosts.

"What's funny?" Gloria asks.

"Ghosts," I say. "I feel like I'm haunted, but I think I could leave my ghost somewhere in the country. Somewhere she's been before where it's open and free."

"Wayne, you are one weird guy," Gregory says, but he's smiling. "I think I know what you mean though."

"I guess I do too," Gloria says. "I used to feel my mother was watching me all the time. Even when I was living on my own. It was like she was right there and any minute she was gonna yell at me."

"I don't understand what youse are saying, Dad," George says.

"I want to take this trip and show you the places your mother and I were happy together. And she'll be with us. Her spirit. I feel like it's inside me. And it feels sad."

"Because she's dead," he says.

"Yes, but maybe, if we visit some of those old places, her spirit will get happy and feel strong enough to go out on its own."

"And then you won't be sad?" George asks.

"If I am, it's my own fault."

"But what if her spirit's made sad by the trip?" he asks.

Before I can answer Gloria is up from her chair, behind me, her arms around my neck. She blows against my ear in the teasing way she did as a child when I was, for that brief time, her father. Before her mother and I separated and I lost the child. She hugs me and speaks to George with her lips almost touching my cheek.

"You and your dad are gonna have so much fun on this trip that Wanda's spirit—your mum's—will have a ball. But . . . but . . . " She pulls away from me and walks over to George and loops an arm around him. "You gotta take somebody else with you."

"You, Gloria. Please come with us," I say.

"Sally!" George shouts.

"Neither," Gloria says. "Sally's too old for all that mountain climbing. She can stay with us. And me, I've got my life here."

"Who then?" I ask.

"Bernice, you dummy," she says. And they laugh, except I seem to be left out of the joke.

"I've hardly spoken to her since the lake swim," I say. "I think she's getting ready for the English Channel."

"Call her," Gloria says. "Just call her."

Later, after Gloria and Gregory have taken small Thomas home to their place and I have George in bed, I think of calling Bernice. She is the same age as Gloria. A child in years and yet I watched her, stroke by stroke, hour after hour until she finally conquered Lake Ontario. Swimming for her life. And maybe that's what frightens me about her. That determined drive. Pushing herself to a limit I can't even imagine. And yet she wants me. Or wants to be with me. We have never made love but when she is with me, her hands or some part of her body, but especially her hands, find a way to make physical contact with me. It's hard to describe how Bernice touches. Some people claw at you, others bump around like river-floating logs. With some people I feel poked at with a sharp stick. But Bernice has a warm, life-giving touch. I've been with her in the swimming pool where she works and had her rub her foot against my bare leg and felt a warm tingle. And the water was cold. It's enough to scare the ghost out of me.

So I have nothing to lose. Except the ghost. I call her.

"You sure you've got the right number," she says.

"I'm sorry . . . "

"Hey, I'm just kidding. I'm thrilled you asked me. Is it okay with George?"

"Sure," I say, thinking I never really asked him. "But what about the Channel? I thought you were going to England."

"The weather's awful," she says. "It's too late in the season. We'll maybe try next year."

"Are you sure you can get time off from the pool?"

She laughs.

"Trying to back out already, eh? No way, Wayne. They owe me the time. But there is one condition."

"What's that?"

"We take my car."

It's my turn to laugh.

"You mean that big beast they gave you for swimming the lake?"

"The beast, as you call it, is a Thunderbird, a very classy car with a great sound system."

"All right. All right, we'll take it. Even if it costs us a zillion dollars for gas. But I get to drive it sometimes."

"You can drive it all the time," she says. "I just like to lounge in it. So, when are we leaving?"

"Tomorrow," I say.

"Doesn't give me much time to get my seduction kit in order, but okay, I'll stay up all night. You're talking three weeks, a month for this trip, so there's a chance sex might creep into the picture, isn't there?"

"Bernice, I've tried to explain. I . . . "

"I know," she says, laughing lightly. "You're sexually taboo. I'm sure we'll work something out on the trip. I'll try my damnedest. Pick you up in the morning."

I am left with the dial-tone and my own trembling reservations.

In the morning as we're packing I try to convey a sense of choice to George about Bernice being on the trip with us. He looks at me earnestly as eight-year-olds sometimes

135

can, takes a deep breath, obviously feeling he has to explain something that he considers to be basic information.

"I like Bernice a lot," he says. "And I think she's the best swimmer in the whole world."

"I like her a lot too," I say, "but I want to make sure that you'll be happy with her along."

"I like her better than you do," he says.

"Why do you say that?"

He looks confused, as if he has no words for something that is just a feeling. I reach for him, hoist him up to my shoulder so he can slide down my back like he used to when he was younger. He laughs and the moment of awkwardness is past.

"Do it again, Dad!" he says. And I do. When he gets up from the carpet he is grinning.

"Bernice gave me a ride in her car already," he says. "You haven't been in it yet."

"True," I say. And maybe after all that's all he was trying to say before, that Bernice had made gestures in his direction that make him feel special. And then she arrives, bouncing with energy into the room, her trim self encased in shorts and a brief pullover. She is wearing a straw hat and outrageous sun-glasses, the frames bright red to match her sandals. She gives George a passing hug and then snuggles provocatively up against me. I can feel her heat.

"Ready fellows," she says in a husky voice.

"Just about," I say, trying to imitate her seductive tone.

I grab some of the bags and head down to the car. I wait there for her to come and open the trunk. A moment to myself. The day is beautiful: a light breeze that tickles the skin, no clouds in the sky and sun warming the earth with a gentle hand. A good day to set out. To move on. I feel a twinge of fear that l will withold myself. I vow to withdraw from the embrace of Wanda's ghost and be open to receive what Bernice offers. And George too. I forget him sometimes.

The two of them come from the house, struggling with the remaining bags, sleeping-rolls, the tent and even the fishing-rods. I rush to help them. It's a feat worthy of a parachute packer to jam all our stuff successfully into the trunk. But finally the lid is closed, with the help of George and Bernice sitting on it. George runs into the house to retrieve a favourite book he has forgotten. Bernice and I face each other.

"We can any of us change our minds whenever we want," she says. "I might get bored with you two and I can always jump on a bus. The same for you. We're not stuck with each other."

"That reminds me," I say. "Did you tell your parents?"

She laughs.

"I brought a note from home."

George reappears and he has Sally with him. The little dog is jumping with excitement as if she thinks she's coming too. I had forgotten her. Gloria said she would come and take her. George has her on the leash and he's wearing a big grin.

"I guess Gloria forgot so Sally's gonna have to come," he says.

I panic for a moment until I see Gloria loping down the hill toward us. She waves. I wave back and marvel at this stranger approaching us who looks so much like me. Another kind of ghost.

"Sorry, guys. Small Thomas was a little cranky this morning. You look ready to go."

"Just waiting for you," I say.

She takes the leash from George's hand, bends and hugs him closely.

"Send me a postcard," she says. "And make your dad have

fun."

"I will," George says. "You look after Sally good. Don't forget she's old."

"I'll take care of her as good as I do small Thomas," she promises.

That satisfies him. He pats Sally one more time and then climbs into the back seat of the car. Gloria moves to Bernice. They embrace, it seems to me, like sisters, sure of each other with some silent and perhaps unstated bond that I do not understand.

"Take care of them," Gloria says. "And don't forget the old one's haunted."

"I'll keep it in mind," Bernice says. "But I think he's harmless."

They disengage and then Gloria turns to me.

"Walk with me for a minute, Dad," she says.

"I'll be in the car," Bernice says.

I walk with Gloria and after a few seconds she takes my hand. Sally walks sedately beside us.

"I'm so glad you're going on this trip," Gloria says. "Especially with Bernice. She cares so much for you. Try to let her give some of it."

"I will," I say, and I mean it.

"I feel so lucky," she says. "I thought I'd lost everything or I'd never have a chance to feel so ... important, I guess. With Gregory, small Thomas. And you, Daddy. Oh, I know you hate that, but sometimes I feel like when I was two or three, just before you left us. You made me feel that everything I did mattered."

"It did to me," I say.

"I knew that then, but I forgot for a long time. Sometimes I hated you, but that wasn't true. It was just that after you left I didn't know who to trust. But now I know, all along it was still you."

She stops and folds herself gently against my chest and I feel her sobs. Why is she crying? She clings to me like a small child. I hold her, I hope gently. Slowly she withdraws, looks up at me and smiles.

"I'm just trying to say that you don't have to prove to me that you're trustworthy. But maybe to yourself. Trust yourself, Dad," she says. And then she turns and walks off, leaving me there feeling kind of stunned. Thankfully, the honking horn pulls me away from wondering what my daughter meant.

That evening we are camped at a provincial park about 50 miles west of Sudbury. I have been here before with Wanda. I even managed to get the same location to pitch our tent. It overlooks a small lake that shines gold in the setting sun. Our tent is up. The sleeping-bags arranged inside, so we each have plenty of space to thrash around. We have cooked and eaten our first meal over an open fire. Darkness begins to close in and the fire dances and sends off sparks. The smoke is a strange comfort.

"Your mum and I toasted marshmallows the night we stayed here," I say to George.

"Can we?" he asks, his voice quiet with fatigue.

"We forgot to bring some. Tomorrow we'll buy a supply."

"Okay," he says and yawns. And then he gets up. "Maybe I'll try laying down."

I tuck him into the sleeping-bag and he is asleep before I leave the tent.

Bernice is sitting at the picnic table poking the fire with a stick. We both watch the explosion of sparks that form instant patterns and then disappear.

"You're thinking of Wanda," she says.

"She liked this place."

"It's beautiful. Like today. I've had a wonderful time, Wayne. What about you?"

"We sure managed to wear out George. He never volunteers to go to bed."

She stands up, looking somehow vulnerable in the dancing shadows from the fire. Her eyes seem so questioning, like a child's. I feel so grateful for her presence. It is like I am less alone, more hopeful about something but I don't know what.

"Walk with me," she says, holding out her hand.

We take the path that leads down to the lake. At the shore she turns her back to me and removes her clothes. When she is naked she turns and smiles. I feel awed and aroused at the same time. It's a strange kind of embarrassment.

"I'm going for a swim," she says. "Join me."

Slowly she disappears into the depths of the water. My hands are moving on my clothes. Something within me is singing. A haunting old song that I will never remember. The same as I will never catch Bernice. But the pull and desire to do so is there. I run into the water. It's cold against my skin. I see Bernice moving smoothly, with her powerful stroke pulling her farther and farther from the shore. I hesitate. And she stops and calls to me across the water and I am surprised at how soft, and even haunting, her voice sounds.

"Swim to me, Wayne," she says. "I'll wait."

And then I dive in and begin my frantic crawl toward her still figure, waiting in the water. Within seconds my arms ache and my breathing is a laboured wheeze. And somewhere within myself I know I'm laughing about this; here I am swimming, moving into deeper and deeper, unknown water, as if my life depended on it.